The Real Thing

By Rosamond Du Jardin:

ROSAMOND DU JARDIN

THE
REAL
THING

A Tobey Heydon Story

J. B. LIPPINCOTT COMPANY

PHILADELPHIA AND NEW YORK

*To Snowbound Lana, who sleeps
in my study while I write*

Contents

The Real Thing

Parting Is Such—

THERE'S JUST ONE TROUBLE WITH SUMMER. IT ZIPS PAST too quickly. But even though you know that's always the case, you get fooled all over again every year. When school's out in June, all those lovely long weeks loom ahead of you, filled with countless days to squander and have fun in and more hours and minutes than you can possibly use up. You figure there'll be loads of time for everything you want to do. And then, without your realizing how it could have happened—wham!—it's September. The endless, lazy summer's past. Oh, you've had fun, of course. But you could have had more fun, done so many more things, gone so many more places, if only you'd known how soon it would be over.

And the very shortest summer of all is the one between a girl's graduation from high school and her entrance into college. I've just learned that from experience.

When I came down to breakfast this morning, wearing my new charcoal gray tweed skirt and the apple-green sweater that I feel does the very most for my coppery hair and brown eyes, my family stared at me in astonishment. I'll admit I don't usually get so dressed up that early, but I resented my mother and father and my young sister, Midge, looking quite so blank about it. After all, even though a girl is more the blue-jeans-and-old-shirt type at breakfast, they should have remembered that this was a very special day.

"Wow!" Midge exclaimed, her eyes widening and her spoon suspended, dripping, over her cereal dish. "What gives?"

Midge is at the difficult age, although with her it seems to be continuing longer than usual. She has sandy braids and a brace on her teeth and even more freckles than I used to have when I was younger, if that's possible. And she looked singularly revolting, sitting there staring at me with her mouth open. I looked away from her deliberately, ignoring her question, and slid into my seat at the other side of the table.

"Dear?" my mother's voice was so questioning, I had to glance up and I found her staring at me almost as blankly as Midge was, but at least Mom's mouth was closed. She asked then, "Isn't that one of the new outfits you're saving for college?"

I nodded, but before I could explain, my father leaned forward, elbow on the table and chin on palm to stare at me approvingly. "I knew it!" he said. "She's growing up. She's old enough to realize at last that the day begins at breakfast and there's no reason to start it off looking like a witch on her way to haunt a house. I'm proud of you, Tobey!"

My father is a dear, but I detected a broad note of sarcasm in that remark. However, I ignored it.

Mom smiled across the table at me, but there was still a question in her eyes. "It's fine to look neat at breakfast," she said, "but if you spill anything, we won't have time to get those clothes cleaned before you start off to Central tomorrow."

"I do not," I said quietly, "intend to spill anything." Honestly, you'd think I was ten years old instead of two whole months over eighteen. I went on, "If you'd stop to think what day this is, you'd realize why I want to look my best."

"Isn't it Wednesday?" Dad asked and I could tell by the worried little way he frowned that he was wondering whether he'd forgotten somebody's birthday or an anniversary or anything.

"It's Wednesday," I admitted. "But it's also the day Brose is leaving for Colorado. He's coming by for me in half an hour, so I can see him off at the train."

"Big deal!" my little sister said, very dead-pan. "I thought it was really some important day, the way you sounded."

"Midge!" Mom's tone was reproving. "It is an important day." She smiled at me in the understanding way she has and I found myself smiling back at her, although I didn't really feel very gay.

Somehow, the realization that Brose was going a thousand miles away from Edgewood to college, while I'd be less than a hundred miles from home at Central University, hadn't hit me full-force until this morning. Even last night, when we'd had our last date and had talked everything over so seriously, our being apart hadn't seemed entirely real.

Last night had been quite an evening. Barbie Walters, my best girl friend, had given a big farewell party and the whole crowd had been there. Everyone was very gay and we'd played records and danced and acted out silly charades and yakked our heads off, just as we always did. If there was a cloud over the party, if the knowledge that this was the last time we'd all be together for quite a while had lurked in the backs of our minds, we wouldn't admit it. Most of us would be going to different colleges, some had decided to try for jobs in bigger towns than Edgewood, a few of the boys were going into service, rather than wait for the draft to get them later on. All of us were aware of these things, but there was no use brooding over them.

Barbie and her charade team didn't help matters any by acting out the quotation, "Parting is such sweet sorrow."

When the party broke up, Brose and I took the long way home and drove around the lake road. Our lake in Edgewood is so small it isn't much good for anything but ice skating in the winter time. It's too muddy to swim in. But just the same, when the moon is high and makes a silvery path across it and the trees all around are sort of dark and whispering and mysterious, it has a certain charm. Brose stopped the car and put his arm around me and we kissed for a long, exciting minute. Brose's kisses have a very disturbing effect on me and it seems to be getting more so rather than less. I could feel his heart pounding and knew he was experiencing similar sensations.

Then he sort of gulped, "Oh, Tobey," in an unhappy tone. And we both leaned back and he put his arm along the top of the seat and I rested my head against it.

"I wish," Brose said, "my father hadn't gone to college in Colorado and didn't have his heart set on my going to the same school. Then I could have gone to Central with you and—"

But I interrupted, because it didn't do any good to

talk like that. "Brose, it's all set. There's nothing we can do now."

"I know." Brose sighed.

"In a way," I went on, "it's really better this way."

"Don't be sensible," Brose begged, "not tonight."

I knew what he meant. We'd talked it all over so many times. We both knew that being apart would give us a chance to meet other people, to decide whether the way we felt about each other was just kid stuff, or the real thing. After all, we'd been a pretty steady twosome during our junior and senior years at high school. Oh, there had been some minor upheavals, of course, when we'd got mad and dated other people for a little while. But we kept getting back together again. And if we went to the same college, I had a pretty good idea we'd keep on the same way. But at different schools, hundreds and hundreds of miles apart, we'd both have the opportunity to grow up some more and find out how a new perspective might affect our relationship.

Brose said, his voice husky, "When I think of not seeing you for almost four months—it does something to me."

There was nothing I could say to cheer him. It would be that long, I knew. He wouldn't be able to get home for Thanksgiving, as I could. We wouldn't see each other again till the Christmas holidays. Four months stretched out as long ahead of us as four years.

So we sat for a little while, talking everything over again, repeating all the things we'd repeated so often before. We were going to write once a week, at least. We'd tell each other all that was happening. But we weren't going to hold off from dating any other people we wanted to. We were going to make new friends and have fun, while we were busy getting educated. Wasn't that what college was for, to help people mature and become independent and learn to make decisions for themselves? Later on, we would decide about us. That was the way we left it.

Brose had driven me home then and I'd come in and gone upstairs and got ready for bed, all in a fine thrilled glow from his good-night kiss. I'd tried to forget it was also a good-bye kiss. And I'd fallen asleep, remembering the feel of his arms around me, not looking ahead at all.

But now it was morning and time had run out completely. I sat there at the table, feeling awful, but trying to make myself eat, so that nobody would remark about my lack of appetite. But there was this tremendous ache of loss that stopped up my throat, so that I could hardly swallow. Mom and Dad and Midge kept talking in a very lively animated manner and I hoped they didn't notice my silence.

After I had choked down some orange juice and half a piece of toast, I jumped up, remarking that the Gilmans would be stopping by for me any minute, so I'd better wait in the front hall. Then I heard the familiar beep of their car horn and hurried out to join them.

Brose's father was driving and Mrs. Gilman sat with him on the front seat. Brose got out and held the back door open politely, then slid in beside me. The Gilmans are nice agreeable people and we all greeted each other cordially. Still, I could tell Brose's parents were feeling rather stricken. He is an only child and for this reason I expect his leaving home for the first time is going to be quite a blow for his parents. In our family it's different. With four girls to divide their time among, two married now, my parents have got sort of used to our comings and goings and are fairly philosophical about separations. Not that they love us any less.

Brose had my hand in his and he looked deep into my eyes without saying anything. He seemed more attractive than usual this morning, his dark hair so crisp and short cut, his eyes sort of brooding and miserable. He was wearing dark brown slacks and a tan tweed sport jacket and I could just imagine the impact he was going to have on all those female wolves out West. My heart sank even lower, which placed it about in the vicinity of my left knee. I sighed deeply.

"Isn't it a lovely morning?" Mrs. Gilman said brightly.

"Oh, yes," I agreed, although I hadn't really noticed.

"Cool for this time of year, though," Mr. Gilman said.

"Oh, yes," I agreed again, curling my fingers closer in Brose's hand.

"I think I'd better park here," Brose's father said, edging the car in to the curb. "It's always so crowded around on the other side and it's only a few steps farther from here."

"Oh, yes," I said. How had we reached the station so soon? It was all of a mile from our house and usually it took much longer.

Mr. and Mrs. Gilman got out of the car. Brose let my hand go and stepped out onto the sidewalk, turning then to help me down as though I were made out of something that might break. The sun was shining brightly and the sky above us was a clear light blue. I felt it would have been much more appropriate if it were raining.

The male Gilmans each took a suitcase out of the car trunk. "Better let me have that big one, son," Mr. Gilman suggested, although Brose is taller than he by a good two inches. But it seems so hard for parents to realize that their children are grown up and able to carry just as heavy loads as they are.

"Don't be silly," Brose said. "I can take them both."

But his father wouldn't let him do that. He lifted the smaller bag and led the way as we all straggled into the station.

It smelled, as always, of dust and smoke in an acrid mixture. Brose bought his ticket and put it away carefully in the new wallet I'd given him for his birthday. Lucky wallet, I thought, to go right along with him.

"Train won't be here for ten minutes," his father said, consulting his watch.

"I know." Brose nodded. "Nine-five, it's due."

Mrs. Gilman pinched a fleck of lint from the shoulder of his jacket. I hadn't even noticed it was there. Her lips were smiling, but her eyes looked desolate. I realized that my lips were turned up stiffly at the corners, too, and I wondered whether my eyes looked as unhappy as Mrs. Gilman's. Just in case they did, I lowered my eyelids to hide them.

"Ambrose," she began and I suspect Brose winced, because she's the only one he'll let get away with calling him that, "when it gets cold out there, remember . . ."

But Brose interrupted, coloring a little, "Aw, now, Mom, cut it out!" He gave her elbow a little affectionate squeeze, though, for being so concerned about his welfare.

What in the world did people talk about during moments like this, I wondered a trifle wildly. I couldn't think of a thing.

Suddenly Brose grabbed my hand and started pulling me along, announcing over his shoulder to his startled parents, "Just remembered I have to make a phone call. Tobey can help me look up the number."

"I'll be glad to—" Mr. Gilman began and then stopped, so abruptly that I felt pretty sure Mrs. Gilman had nudged his arm.

The phones were around the corner. It was a tight squeeze for us both in the booth and we left the door a little open, so the light didn't go on. Brose held me hard against him and kissed me and I co-operated fully. I was glad I'd bitten off most of my lipstick, trying to keep my lips from trembling. It didn't smudge him at all. "Good-bye, Tobey," he whispered.

"Oh, Brose." I gulped, "I'll miss you so—" I couldn't go on, but I gave him a look positively dripping with meaning.

We heard the train coming then, so we raced back to join his parents. Brose kissed his mother and shook hands with his father and gave my shoulders a tight, final squeeze. There was a flurry of good-byes as we moved out to the platform. Then Brose was on the train and the conductor was calling, "Bo-aarrdd." The train pulled out deafeningly.

"Well," Mr. Gilman said heavily, "well—"

"Oh, dear," Mrs. Gilman quavered, fishing in her purse for a hanky.

I was glad when she found it, because I didn't have a spare, and I was going to have to blow my nose, too.

"Now, Mother," Mr. Gilman soothed. "We'll be going out to see him in November."

I wouldn't see him till Christmas vacation. I just stood there and ached. If it hadn't been that I'd be leaving for college myself tomorrow, I don't think I could have borne it.

two

Last Day

As usual, i'd left a thousand and one things to do at the last minute. But in this particular instance, I was glad I had. Whenever I thought of Brose, getting farther away from me every hour, I felt weepy. So it was just as well there wasn't much time for brooding.

I was in the throes of packing when Barbie Walters stopped by for a minute. Mom sent her up to my room and Barbie perched on the edge of my bed and surveyed the stacks of undies and hangers full of dresses and layers of blouses and sweaters and skirts with a sympathetic eye. Barbie is cute and perky, with dark hair and a sense of humor. Her harlequin glasses have bright blue frames this year, which gives her a dash of sophistication. Barbie and I have been best friends so long, we have no secrets from each other. The only reason we didn't pick the same college was that Barbie wanted a school with a stronger art department than Central has. She plans to major in dress design.

She informed me, nodding airily at my scattered wardrobe, "I just conquered a mess like this. How it all went into two suitcases and a trunk, I'll never know.

But I'm a living, breathing example that it can be done. Don't let me interrupt you."

"Thanks for the inspiration," I said drily and stood there with a pair of pajamas in one hand and several pairs of white ankle socks in the other, trying to decide where to put them.

"Corners," Barbie advised sagely. "Roll things up and stick them in corners. They don't seem to take up so much room that way."

I tried it and it worked. I began stuffing things into corners like crazy. Maybe I could take along everything I wanted to, after all. If I could cram all the little stuff into my suitcases, that would leave my new wardrobe trunk to hold all the dresses and suits and things I didn't want to crush.

"Did you see the Man off?" Barbie asked.

"Don't remind me." I sighed.

"I'm glad Sox and I broke up for keeps," Barbie confided. "The glow was gone, and this way I can look ahead to all the men I'm going to meet at college with a clear conscience."

"My conscience is clear, too," I told her. "Brose and I talked everything over and we agreed it would be silly for us to feel we had any strings on each other. We're both perfectly free to date anyone we want to."

"That's good," Barbie said. "I hoped you had too much sense to do anything else. Why, just think, Tobey," her tone grew dreamy, "college will be a whole new world for us. All new people, different surroundings, experiences we've never had before. It'll be like a new sheet of white paper, on which we can write anything we like—I read that somewhere. But isn't it an exciting thought? I can hardly wait!"

I nodded. It was exciting when you considered it. Here in Edgewood, most of my friends had known me forever. They knew the kind of grades I got in school and remembered when I used to wear braces on my teeth and were fairly sure how I'd react in any given situation. There was nothing new about me, no mystery. And I couldn't change my personality very much without having everyone notice and think I was posing, not being myself.

But at college no one would know me well enough to make me feel I had to follow the same pattern I had at home. Oh, a few acquaintances were going to Central, but none of my really intimate friends. Of course, my sister Alicia would be there and her husband, Adam Wentworth, who was studying to be a doctor. But the married students stuck together pretty much; their activities and interests were different from those of the single crowd. Alicia had told me that herself. I didn't expect I'd be seeing very much of her and Adam, even though I was going to drive to school with them tomorrow morning.

"I'm planning," Barbie's voice broke in on my reflections, "to change my name."

"Your name?" I gasped. "But—how can you?"

"Perfectly simple," Barbie said. "I signed my application with my full name, Barbara Carolyn Walters. That gives me a lot of leeway. I can be Caro Walters, or Lynn Walters, or at least Barb." She added disgustedly, "Barbie sounds about six years old and I've been getting sicker and sicker of it."

I could see what she meant. "Seems like a good idea."

"How about you?" Barbie began. But then a light of realization broke over her face and I knew she was remembering that Tobey was my middle name and that my first one was Henrietta, after my father. "No," Barbie said drily, "I guess not. You'd better stay Tobey."

"I intend to," I told her. "But let me know which you decide on, so I'll know how to address your letters."

We talked for a little while longer, as I went on with my packing. This was the last time we'd see each other, since Barbie, too, would be leaving early the next morning. And both of us felt that our last evening at home should be reserved for our families.

"Well," Barbie said finally, "I have to get going. Have fun at school and be sure to remember all the fascinating details you can't put down on paper, for when we get together at Thanksgiving."

"You, too," I told her.

I went down to the front door with her, both of us locked in an unnatural silence. We gave each other a little self-conscious hug in the lower hall and said good-bye. My mother came out of the kitchen to tell Barbie good-bye, too, and wish her luck.

As Barbie left, she called back, I suppose from force of habit, "Be seeing you."

Only we wouldn't be seeing each other, I realized glumly, not for quite a long while.

"You two will miss each other," Mom said, as she headed back for the kitchen, where, I knew, she was busy preparing all my favorite foods for dinner. "You've been together so much."

"Yeah," I nodded. I watched Barbie out of sight beyond our hedge and then went rather slowly back upstairs to finish my packing. I was glad I had something to do, but I was beginning to wish tomorrow would hurry up and come.

Dinner was wonderful, as I had known it would be. Swiss steak, as only Mom can make it, with all the trimmings. And my favorite torte, smothered in strawberries and whipped cream, for dessert. Alicia and Adam were there and so was Adam's father, who is a widower and owns the best department store in Edgewood. We were all very talkative and gay, but there was the same little undercurrent of sadness that I had detected at Barbie's farewell party. The knowledge that this was our final time together for a while had to be kept pushed far enough back in our minds so that it wouldn't spoil our evening.

And it didn't. We had a lot of fun. But after the others had left and Mom and Dad and Midge and I were on our way upstairs, Midge said, voicing all our thought, I guess, "It was a real cool party—only—I was too sort of unhappy inside to enjoy it."

Mom gave her a little hug.

And Dad said, trying to keep things light, "At least, you got to stay up a lot later than usual."

Midge nodded. "I know. But—I didn't think I was going to feel bad, having Tobey go."

"I'm not going very far, honey," I told her. How can little sisters be such blights and then turn around and say something so sweet you feel like kissing them? "I'll get home for a week end every now and then." I laid my hand on her shoulder and gave it a little squeeze and she grinned up at me a shade doubtfully.

"Of course you can," Mom said heartily, almost too heartily.

And Dad added, "She'll probably be back so often we'll be sick of seeing her." But he didn't sound at all as if he meant it.

What could we say to each other? I couldn't tell them they were the two most wonderful parents in the world and that I was going to miss them, and even Midge, like the very dickens. And they couldn't come right out and say they hated to see me go, that the three of them were going to rattle around in our big old house like the last peas left in the pod, and that having one more child leave home, even if only to go to college, was quite a blow.

"Think," I pointed out with a little giggle, "how much less strain there'll be on the shower and the phone with me gone!"

That made them laugh and cleared the air somewhat. We all said good night and drifted off to bed. But I couldn't fall asleep right away, much as I needed to since Alicia and Adam would be picking me up early in the morning.

Go to sleep! I thought firmly. Other girls go to college. Why are you making such a Big Thing of it?

As my eyes accustomed themselves to the dark, I found myself looking around my familiar room, trying to impress every single detail on my memory. It's funny how inanimate objects can become entangled in your mind with different happenings in your life. That was the dressing table at which I'd sat to apply my first lipstick, one I'd snitched from my oldest sister, Janet. There was the closet in which my first formal had hung. This was the bed on which I'd flung myself to cry when I'd broken up with Brose. And underneath me was the mattress beneath which I had hidden my diary to keep it away from Midge's inquiring eyes—only she'd managed to find it anyway. Trust Midge!

By this time tomorrow I'd be sleeping in a different bed, in totally strange surroundings. What would they be like, I wondered? I had only seen Mercer Hall, the freshman girls' dormitory at Central, from the outside. And I knew that during Rush Week, until you were pledged to a sorority and moved into a sorority house, Mercer was where you stayed. Because of there being so many girls who hoped to pledge a club, you were crowded in, three to a room. If you didn't make a sorority, you stayed on at Mercer. And maybe, I reminded myself, I wouldn't be asked to pledge. Quite a lot of girls missed out. It would be a disappointment, of course, but I didn't intend to let a thing like that throw me.

I lay there, thinking about college and sororities and all the new people I was going to meet. I wondered who my roommates at Mercer would be, whether we'd be congenial and like each other, or get in each other's hair. Three in a room could be a problem, I imagined, even for a week. Or it could be fun. By this time tomorrow I should have some idea.

Rather foggily, just before I fell asleep, it struck me that at some point since I'd gone to bed, the whole direction of my thinking had changed. I was looking ahead, rather than back, wondering about tomorrow, rather than brooding over today and yesterday. Oh, I'd miss Brose and my family, all my old friends. I still knew that. But the knowledge was less sharp and hurting, wrapped as it was now in layers of excited anticipation of what lay ahead. If I dreamed, I thought drowsily, it would be about college.

And sure enough, it was. I dreamed I went to my first class and didn't discover till I had sat down right next to the most attractive boy in the room that I had left my hair up in pin curls and was wearing a shapeless old tee-shirt and blue jeans. Then he turned around and laughed in my face and, surprisingly, he was Brose Gilman. Only he looked at me as though he had never seen me before and wouldn't listen when I tried to tell him who I was. All night long, I kept on trying to persuade him that we were old friends, who used to date each other all the time.

I was glad when I woke up and saw the sun shining through my window and realized, my heart quickening, that this was The Day. The hands of my alarm clock stood at seven-twenty. I had beaten it to the draw by ten minutes. In about an hour Adam would honk for me and he and Alicia and I would take off. Adam and Dad had loaded all my luggage into the car trunk last night, so we wouldn't be delayed.

While I packed I had wondered whether to wear my Black Watch plaid skirt and green sweater, or my charcoal tweed suit. First impressions were so important and I wanted to look my best from the very moment I arrived at college. I had finally decided on the suit, as it made me look a little older. Excitement and anticipation welled up in me like a fountain and I leaped out of bed, smiling. This is definitely not my usual method of arising.

In what seemed like no time at all, I had showered and dressed. Breakfast was over in a rush, with my parents practically overwhelming me with last minute instructions and warnings. Be sure to keep your checking account balanced and let us know when you need more money in it. Don't stay up too late, you must get your rest, dear. Have fun, but remember you are going to college for an education. Grades are important, too. And do write, as often as you can.

"Write me, too," Midge said, rather unexpectedly. "I mean me by myself, some personal private letters."

I agreed to everything, nodding and smiling, loving them all to death. Then Adam's car horn beeped on the drive and I kissed everybody and ran out to join Alicia and Adam.

Central, here I come! I thought exultantly.

three

Roommates

THERE IS A SORT OF MAGIC IN THE VERY WORDS RUSH WEEK. At least that's the way I felt about it. Maybe it isn't every girl's dream to go to college and join a sorority, but it certainly was one of my fond hopes. I'd had a tiny tantalizing taste of sorority life last year when Dick Allen invited me to Central for a football week end and dance and I'd stayed with Geri Clair at the Theta house. That had been such fun and I'd liked the girls I'd met so well. Geri had promised to put in a good word for me with the Thetas when I came to college. Not, I knew, that the influence of one friend who was a member could get you in. It was by no means that simple.

Alicia had laid a bit of groundwork for me, too, with her sorority, the Tau Kappas. "But don't count on being pledged," she warned me that morning as we drove toward Central through the sunny September day. "I understand we have more legacies than we can handle this year. And I don't carry too much weight around the house since I married and moved out. I'll do what I can for you at Hash Session, though."

"What are Hash Sessions like?" I asked, a little scared

at the mere thought of being discussed and decided about by the regular sorority members.

"Barbarous," Adam stated flatly.

"Now, honey," Alicia demurred, "you've never been to one."

The idea of my very masculine brother-in-law at a sorority session of any sort made me smile. Adam, too, grinned at the incongruity of it. Still he insisted, "I know they're barbarous, just from what I've heard about them."

Alicia asked, with a little shrug, "How else can we decide who we'll take in? Can you think of a better system?"

"I couldn't figure out a worse one," Adam argued. "It's crazy. First you throw some big parties for the rushees, give them the full red-carpet treatment. Then the regulars get together after the potential pledges have gone home and tear them to shreds. And you don't even know most of them well enough to decide whether they'll make good members or not. How can you, after just a couple of teas and a big dinner party?"

"It is hard," Alicia admitted, frowning. "And you have to consider so many angles, too. Some years, when we haven't had a Beauty Queen for a while, we decide to concentrate on pledging only the prettiest girls. Other times, when our scholastic average gets shaky, it's brains that count. And there are always some legacies we just can't get out of accepting, no matter what pots they are."

"But how can you possibly decide intelligently?" Adam asked. "You've probably only seen them a couple of times yourself, when they were stiff and self-conscious, scared half to death at a Rush Tea or something, trying to make a good impression. And on that skimpy basis you decide which ones should get the axe!"

"You sound as if it's all my fault!" My sister's blue eyes had begun to sparkle angrily, a danger signal I recognized.

But Adam was too intent on his own train of thought to notice. "The bad part is, some of these crazy freshmen take it dead seriously. If they aren't asked to pledge the sorority they've set their hearts on, it can affect their whole lives, wreck their self-confidence, make them feel rejected."

"Well, don't berate me," Alicia snapped. "I didn't invent the Hash Session, or sororities, either!"

I put in hastily, feeling that a little oil on the troubled waters would be a good idea, "I don't care enough one way or the other to let it make me really miserable if I'm not asked to pledge. Oh, I'd like to join a sorority, of course. But I'll live if I don't get to—and enjoy myself, too," I added lightly.

Actually, I would rather have a chance to join the Thetas than the Tau Kappas, but I saw no reason to go into that with Alicia. Maybe it was unreasonable of me, since the Taus were a larger and more influential club than the Thetas. But I still remembered the old Southern Colonial charm of the big red-brick Theta house and the friendliness of Geri and the others. The whole warm, easy, unpretentious atmosphere had appealed to me strongly.

"Attagirl," Adam said. "Now you're talking sense. At Central the independents are almost as active as the Greek letter clubs, anyway. It's just that sororities and fraternities have a certain snob appeal that dazzles some people."

"If you mean me—" Alicia began indignantly.

But Adam interrupted, "I don't, baby. I'm just generalizing. The clubs have their place, I suppose. But that doesn't mean they couldn't stand more improvement. Right?" His grin was conciliatory.

After a minute, Alicia returned it. "Right," she said.

They are really cute, the way they're always getting into terrific hassles and then calming down and making up again. I guess that's just the way marriage is.

Central has a lovely campus, sort of hilly and rolling, with lots of big old trees and buildings ranging from mellowed and almost shabby to modern and functional, with lots of windows, but not so much charm. I had always thought it beautiful, but now I had a lot warmer and more personal feeling about it. Now it was My School and I looked at the people strolling along the winding walks and clustering on the broad steps with a little feeling of kinship beginning to glow in me. Would that girl with the blond pony tail ever become my friend? Would I have a date sometime with the tall boy who was taking the steps to the Administration Building three at a time? Would that bespectacled, bald man, obviously a professor, ever give me a hard time with an unexpected test?

The car slid to a stop in front of one of the newer buildings and Adam broke into my thoughts by saying, "Well, here we are. You and I can register, Tobey, and then we'll drop you and your stuff off at Mercer."

"I'll wait in the car," Alicia said, settling back cozily. "But get through as fast as you can. I'm dying to get over to our place and see how they decorated it."

The quonset in which Alicia and Adam first lived at college has finally been replaced by a regular apartment building. All the married students are much more com-

fortable in their new quarters, although Alicia and Adam
still don't have room for some of their wedding gifts,
such as the grandfather clock which Adam's elderly
Aunt Tess wished on them.

I went with my brother-in-law up a flight of stone
steps and through a heavy door into a brightly lit interior.
People stood in line at several registration desks and
there was a murmur of politely muted conversation.

"You sign up over there." Adam aimed me in the
right direction. "That's Freshman Registration. I'll be
over here in the senior line. It shouldn't take too long."

The registrars worked with calm efficiency and the lines
moved along briskly. Soon it was my turn to answer the
questions on an official-looking form. Name, address,
age and so on. When the form had been all filled in, I
was assigned to Room 210 in Mercer Hall for the
duration of Rush Week and given a nod and a dis-
missing smile. I stepped aside and stood there, waiting
for Adam. People were milling all about. I tried to decide which of them were freshmen like myself and was
surprised at how easily you could tell. We all had an
awed, uncertain manner, while the upperclassmen
seemed to be taking the whole dull routine business
in stride. I felt a little better. At least there were others
in the same boat with me.

"Okay." My brother-in-law came up finally. "Guess
we're all set. We'll dump you at Mercer on our way
home."

"Fine," I replied, turning the corners of my mouth up
in what I hoped was a nonchalant smile. A queer hollow
feeling grew inside of me at the prospect of being de-
serted by my sister and Adam, left on my own. But I

tried to ignore it and think ahead to my imminent meeting with my two roommates.

Mercer was a big, squarish building with a drive that went around in a semi-circle on the wide lawn in front of it. Adam got a janitor to help him with my trunk and suitcases and I introduced myself to the tall efficient-looking girl who was on duty in the entrance hall to direct new-comers to their rooms.

She said her name was Linda Beldon and she was glad to see me and my room was on the second floor, three doors to the left along the hall. Her smile was friendly enough, but her voice sounded rather like a phonograph record. She'd probably been saying the same thing to so many people she didn't have to think about the words anymore, only to substitute the right name and room location.

"Well, so long, kid," Adam said, giving me a casual, big brotherly sort of hug as we met at the foot of the stairs, he coming down and me starting up. "We'll be giving you a ring soon, getting together."

I nodded and thanked him and said, "So long, be seeing you." The front door thudded shut behind him as he hurried out to join Alicia. There were two of them and only one of me. I felt utterly forlorn and alone, in spite of the muffled voices seeping from rooms all about.

The door of Number 210 was partly open. Just inside I saw my luggage piled up and it gave me a slightly homey feeling. It, at least, was familiar. The room was light blue as to walls and limed oak as to furniture. There were twin beds and an extra cot, all covered in gay chintz spreads that matched the curtains. No one seemed to be around but me. I advanced farther into the room, my glance exploring it. If I was the first occupant to arrive, I might as well make myself at home and begin to get settled.

Suddenly a door across the room burst open and I started in surprise. A very pretty girl with blond hair and wide, appalled brown eyes stood in the bathroom doorway, staring at my luggage. She wore a tweed skirt and a frilly white blouse, only partially buttoned. Her feet were bare and she had a pair of high-heeled brown suede pumps in one hand.

Before I could speak she lifted her eyes from my trunk to look straight at me. Then she said accusingly, "It was your trunk they brought in! I was taking a bath and I heard them set it down and I was sure it must be mine. We sent it three days ago and it should have got here before I did—only it didn't. And I haven't any clothes with me except what I have on and I thought, of course, when I heard someone setting down a trunk that it just had to be mine. How in the world," she demanded, frowning, "did yours get here so soon when you just came yourself?"

"I—we—that is my sister and her husband and I brought it with us," I explained apologetically. "We drove."

"Oh," she said. She sat down on the edge of one of the beds and buttoned up the rest of her blouse.

After a moment's uneasy silence, I told her, "I'm Tobey Heydon."

"I'm Marilyn Jennings," she said, "from Detroit. How could it possibly take a trunk so long to go a few hundred miles? If I'd had any idea, we could have sent it sooner, but I didn't want things to just lie in it and get crushed till I got here. Oh, it's so awful!"

I nodded sympathetically. It would be a blow to arrive at college, expecting your clothes to be there by the time you were and then find out they weren't. "If I can lend you anything—" I began.

But Marilyn said impatiently, "You're too short. Your things wouldn't fit me at all."

She made me feel like a midget. I thought it might have been a little more tactful if she'd said she was too tall rather than the other way around. But she was upset, so I made allowances.

"I'm sorry," I told her.

I wasn't sure whether she heard me or not.

After a long moment, she exploded unhappily. "I could simply die! It's so terribly important to look your very best for Rush and I selected my clothes so carefully."

"Your trunk will surely get here today or tomorrow." I tried to comfort her.

"Why?" Marilyn demanded. "If it isn't here yet, it could be lost. Something *must* have happened to it. Why, it could be missent thousands of miles away! I might never get it! All those lovely clothes—" She drew a deep, shaken breath. "And the first Rush Teas start tomorrow."

I knew that. Still, at the risk of getting snapped at again, I reminded, "They go on through most of next week, though. And surely before then—"

I broke off at the sound of brisk footsteps approaching. The door of our room was still open and now it framed a girl in a trim gray suit, whose dark hair was brushed back smoothly, almost severely, from a pleasant, intelligent, but not really pretty face.

"Hi," she said, smiling first at me and then at Marilyn. "I'm Suz Herrick. I guess we're all roommates."

"Hi," I said, feeling the warmth and friendliness of her smile wrap itself around me in the most ice-breaking fashion. I told her my name and said, "This is Marilyn Jennings."

Marilyn nodded, still frowning. Her glance indicated clearly that she would have greatly preferred Suz to be an expressman bringing her elusive trunk. I couldn't help feeling a touch of annoyance with her for giving our other roommate such a lukewarm welcome and carrying on so over an accident that might have happened to anyone.

Don't make snap judgments, I warned myself sternly. It isn't fair.

But such advice was hard to follow. Suz I was sure I was going to like very much. About Marilyn I didn't feel nearly so certain.

four

Rush Week

ALL DAY FRIDAY AND PART OF SATURDAY WE HAD PLACE-
ment tests. I could think of lots more pleasant ways to
spend my time, although actually they weren't too horrible. They didn't cause anyone to fail, or anything
drastic like that. They simply served to establish the
student's capabilities and intelligence, so that we could
be grouped with others able to learn at approximately
the same speed. We all got pretty sick of these tests
just the same. Still, there were rush parties to look forward to every evening.

"Like a carrot on a string, dangling in front of a hard-
working donkey," was the way Suz put it. She had a droll
sense of humor that I got a big bang out of. But Marilyn
took everything connected with rushing so deadly
seriously, she didn't even want to joke about it.

When our bids to teas and dinner parties and buffet
suppers started coming in, Marilyn was reduced to tears
because her trunk was still missing. She took it as a
personal affront on the part of Fate that such a thing
should have happened to her, rather than to Suz or me.

"You wouldn't have minded nearly as much," she

accused me, "and neither would Suz. You just don't feel the same way I do about sororities."

"Of course we'd mind," I argued. "Nobody wants to get left high and dry during Rush without their best clothes. But the railroad's tracing your trunk. It's sure to turn up soon. And your suit's lovely and perfectly appropriate for teas and Suz and I have both said you can borrow any of our blouses. She even offered you first choice of her dinner dresses for tonight."

This was Saturday and all three of us had been invited to the Tau Kappa dinner party. Marilyn and I had just got back from a tea, but Suz hadn't returned yet from her afternoon party. She and Marilyn were near enough in size, so that Suz's clothes fit Marilyn very well and I thought Suz had been more than generous with her. Maybe Marilyn was really grateful, although she was so completely self-centered, she seemed to accept any favors one did for her as her due and never sounded too whole-hearted in her appreciation.

"I know." She nodded, frowning, "but Suz's clothes— well, they just don't do anything for me! They're so— plain."

"Suz is the tailored type," I reminded, trying to keep the annoyance I felt from sharpening my tone. "She looks her best in simple, unfrilly things. After all, she didn't buy her clothes to suit you."

Marilyn shrugged. "Frankly, I don't think they do much for her either, tailored type or not." Before I could open my mouth to leap to Suz's defense, she went on, "But, of course, I appreciate her helping me out. It's just that if your things would fit me, they'd be so much more becoming. And I do want to look my very best tonight."

She sounded so utterly miserable that I felt my annoyance with her drain away and sympathy seep in to take its place. "You mean you'd rather impress the Taus than the other sororities?"

"Well, of course," Marilyn said. Her tone implied that my question had been unnecessarily stupid. "The Tau Kappas are *the* sorority at Central. Everyone knows that!"

I smiled faintly, pointing out, "I should think it's just a matter of which one you prefer, which group of girls you happen to feel most at home and at ease with."

But Marilyn shook her head positively, as though I were being quite childish and unreasonable. "The Taus are the most outstanding girls on campus," she informed me, "the best-looking, the richest, the ones who really amount to a lot. Why, take yesterday," she went on, "that tea at the Theta House. It was such a slap-dash sort of an affair. But tonight the Taus will have every detail just perfect. You'll see."

"I like the Thetas," I said firmly. "They're so easy to be with, so nice and friendly."

It had been a lovely tea, I thought. Geri had been there and a lot of other girls I'd met last year. They had made me feel warmly welcome, as though they truly liked me and might enjoy having me as a member. They had treated Marilyn cordially, too, although apparently their friendliness had been wasted on her. It had seemed to me that she was more herself with them, more relaxed and natural in her manner than usual. At some of the other parties it had struck me that she was trying too hard to be gay and attractive.

"Oh, they're friendly enough," Marilyn conceded. "I haven't anything against them. But they're just not the cream of the crop the way the Taus are. You'll see the difference at the dinner tonight. And I've heard the Tau house is so lovely. Why, the Thetas' furniture was almost shabby. Didn't you notice that worn spot on the hall rug? And some of their drapes are quite sun faded."

"No, I didn't notice," I said rather shortly. "I guess I was just too busy enjoying myself."

How could some people attach such importance to purely material things. I wondered? I was annoyed enough really to light into Marilyn, but the door behind me opened just then and Suz appeared, interrupting our conversation. She had been at a Rush Tea at a sorority clear down at the other end of the campus. She looked neat and well-scrubbed in a navy wool dress that was quite plain except for the crisp white collar winging out at her throat. She tossed aside her unobtrusive little hat and white gloves and kicked off her high-heeled pumps before she had advanced two steps into the room.

"Murder!" she exclaimed, slumping onto the nearest chair to massage her instep and smile ruefully at Marilyn and me. "These fancy parties are *not* my meat! Why I decided to go through Rush, I'll never know. All this getting dressed up in hats and heels and white gloves— it's getting me down!"

"Why did you decide to?" Marilyn asked curiously. "Somehow or other, you don't seem exactly the sorority type."

"I take that as a compliment at the moment." Suz's tone was dry. "That bunch of would-be sophisticates I just had tea with was enough to sour a sensible person on the whole idea. And I'm nothing if not a sensible person. But I suppose it isn't fair to condemn all sororities on the basis of a few."

"Wait till tonight," Marilyn said dreamily. "Wait till you meet the Taus, although—" she broke off.

I had a pretty good idea she'd been going to finish her sentence, "although it isn't very likely they'll ask you to join." But even Marilyn wouldn't be quite that tactless.

From the look on Suz's face, though, I suspected she'd got Marilyn's meaning. I put in, to fill the rather empty silence, "The Thetas are the ones I like best so far. I'm keeping my fingers crossed, hoping they'll ask me to pledge."

"You'll find there's simply no comparison," Marilyn insisted, "between them and the Taus." And then she added, in a wistful wallow of self-pity, "Oh, I do wish my clothes would come, so that I could look the way I want to tonight."

I wished they would, too, if only so we could stop hearing her carry on about them.

But Suz asked patiently, "Have you decided what you want to borrow, in case they don't turn up?"

"How about your black faille evening skirt?" Marilyn suggested. Then, at Suz's agreeing nod, she turned toward me. "And I thought maybe you'd let me take one of your dressy blouses, say the white lace? It would be more becoming to me than anything of Suz's."

"Okay," I said.

Marilyn smiled sweetly at Suz and me, not even bothering to murmur a word of appreciation.

When we three were dressed for the Tau Kappa dinner party, I thought we made quite an effective contrast for each other. Suz wore gray velveteen, well-cut and probably expensive, but so simple it gave her almost a Puritan air. My emerald green taffeta was quite becoming, making my skin look whiter and my hair more coppery than usual. And Marilyn was beautiful in Suz's skirt and my lace blouse. I don't really think she would have looked any prettier in her own clothes, but she was definitely not satisfied with the effect. She fussed so endlessly with every little detail and complained so bitterly that she had Suz and me about ready to flip with exasperation.

Finally I exploded, "For Pete's sake, Marilyn, come on! You look fine. After all, this isn't a presentation at the royal court, you know. It's just another sorority party."

"Just!" Marilyn repeated in an appalled little gasp. "Tobey, you know how important the Tau Kappas are. Tonight means everything to me. If I don't make a good enough impression so that they ask me to pledge, I'll just die!"

"You're foolish to take any one club so seriously," Suz told her gently, "to set your heart on it that way."

Marilyn shrugged. "Maybe, but that's the way I feel. Tonight's the night, so far as I'm concerned. The Taus just have to want me."

Suz's troubled glance met mine as Marilyn turned back toward the mirror for one last reassuring look at herself. I couldn't help worrying a bit over the crazy kid, too. But what could anyone do?

The Tau Kappa House seemed rather showy and pretentious to me. I much preferred the more casual atmosphere of the Theta House. But Marilyn was obviously dazzled with the expensively formal perfection of the furnishings, the thick pile of the rugs, the interior-decorator choice of colors. Dinner was delicious and the long tables in the big dining room sparkled with white linen and tall maroon candles in silver holders and dark red floral centerpieces. After we'd eaten, the Taus sang sorority songs for us, then took us back into the tastefully appointed lounge where we settled down for an evening of talk and getting acquainted. Alicia was there and she helped make things seem less stiff and formal for me. She tried to see that Suz and Marilyn had a good time, too. Suz was her usual quiet, droll self, her attitude seeming to proclaim, "This is the way I am, take me or leave me." But it seemed to me that Marilyn, who was most anxious of us three to make a good impression, wasn't being herself at all. Maybe she couldn't, under the circumstances. She talked too vivaciously, laughed too much, and her facial expression grew strained with constant smiling. Even her movements seemed forced and theatrical. But maybe, I told myself, this was the way to impress the Taus.

They struck me as rather a snobbish, affected crowd, except for Alicia and a few others. Their clothes were as expensively lovely as the furnishings of their house and there seemed to be a glaze of brittle poise and sophistication upon them that was almost visible. I wasn't enjoying myself very much and, when I caught Suz's eye, it seemed to me she shared my sensations. But Marilyn was in a seventh heaven of delight with everything she saw and heard. I remembered again her voice saying, "If I don't make a good enough impression so that they ask me to pledge, I'll just die." And a little shiver ran down my spine. Maybe, I tried to reassure myself, she was making a good impression. But I didn't think so. . . .

Sunday Suz and I went to Chapel. It wasn't required until the following week, but we both felt like going.

Marilyn was still sound asleep when we left our cluttered room at Mercer. She looked so young and defenseless lying there, her fair hair spread forward fanlike under her cheek, that neither Suz nor I had the heart to waken her.

We strolled along toward the old graystone building, set high on a hill, its white spire pointing skyward.

"Do you suppose she'll make the Taus?" Suz asked me, her tone anxious, and I knew our thoughts had been following the same track.

I shook my head. "I don't know—but she'll certainly be sunk if she doesn't."

"Crazy kid," Suz said, sounding as if she were forty herself. "What she sees in that bunch of superior-acting little snobs—"

I said, "They certainly didn't impress me as a club I'd want to join."

"Me, either." Suz's tone was curiously regretful. "The funny thing is, though, it's the Taus or nothing for me, too, Tobey."

I stared at her blankly. "What do you mean?"

"I'm a solid legacy," Suz said. "My mother's president of the Tau Kappa alums and my grandmother was one of the founding members back in 1800 and something." Her mouth twisted. "I don't think Gran would be very proud, though, if she saw what this particular chapter of her club has developed into. Nor would Mother. But I couldn't very well pledge another sorority under the circumstances, even if I'm asked. So you know what I've decided?"

I shook my head.

"I'm going to drop out of Rush. Last night finished

me. As Marilyn put it, I guess I'm just not the sorority type anyway."

"But there are other clubs that aren't like the Taus—" I began. Still, I could see her position. Coming from a long line of Taus, she couldn't very well break with tradition by joining another sorority. Better just not to pledge at all.

"I know," Suz said, smiling. "And I hope the one you like best asks you to come in. Frankly, I think I'm going to prefer staying independent. But we won't let that spoil our friendship."

"Of course not," I assured her, and meant it.

During the prayer in Chapel, I said a few words in my heart for Marilyn. And I shouldn't be surprised if Suz did the same.

five

Pledge Bids

DURING THE NEXT FEW DAYS THERE WERE SO MANY RUSH parties, they all sort of ran together in my mind into a mad confusion of noisy chatter, clinking tea cups and endless silver platters of fancy cookies. And back at Mercer when we had a few spare moments to kick off our high heels and toss aside our hats and white gloves, how did we relax? By talking about the parties we'd been to and speculating about those we had yet to attend. Oh, it was gay!

Marilyn's wandering trunk arrived on Monday. This made life easier for Suz and me, as well as for her. She did have lovely clothes and I couldn't really blame her for being so upset over the threat of losing them.

But instead of just being grateful, she went on bewailing the fact that they hadn't turned up sooner. "If only I'd been able to dress decently for the Tau party," she lamented. "That was when I really wanted to make the best impression."

She simply could not understand Suz's decision to drop out of Rush entirely. When Suz began politely declining party invitations, Marilyn accused, "You're just crazy! Why on earth would anyone start Rush and then quit cold?"

"Maybe," Suz said with her droll smile, "I'm just one who likes to trade horses in the middle of a stream. You said yourself I didn't seem like the sorority type. I've begun to realize it, too, since I've been here."

She had asked me not to tell anyone else her real reason for changing her mind. And I felt sure the true explanation would have been even less comprehensible to Marilyn than the line Suz was handing her.

"Besides," Suz went on in her half-serious, half-kidding tone, "I've grown so attached to dear old Mercer Hall, I just can't bear the thought of leaving and moving into a sorority house."

I reminded Marilyn, "For that matter, we may all end up staying here. We can't absolutely count on being asked to pledge."

Marilyn looked sick at the mere possibility. "Don't say things like that," she pleaded. "Why, as long as I can remember, I've dreamed of belonging to a sorority. And ever since I got here," she admitted, "I've known that Tau Kappa was the sorority for me. They've just got to want me!"

Her brown eyes were wide and vulnerable and her whole face was intent with hope and expectation. What could you do for anyone with such a stubborn, one-track mind?

Regular classes were scheduled to start on Thursday and a tide of freshmen girls who weren't going through Rush began to wash over Mercer Hall. The big dorm became much more crowded, but only temporarily. By Thursday evening a lot of us rushees would have been asked to pledge and would move at once into various sorority houses. Then life around Mercer would settle down to normal; permanent rooms would be assigned and the frantic confusion of Rush would be over for another year.

Wednesday night was the grand finale of all the rushing parties. Even after the lights had been turned out at Mercer, an excited hum of whispered conversation hung over the place, punctuated by the gnawing sound of fingernails being bitten. Luckily, I didn't dream that night, or I would surely have had nightmares.

When I awoke to the insistent call of my alarm clock, it was with an almost fatalistic sense of peace. All the Hash Sessions were over, I told myself philosophically. Everything was decided. I wouldn't know until late afternoon whether I'd made a sorority or not, but somehow it didn't even seem too important any more. I wasn't quite sure whether it was relief I was experiencing, or if I was just numb.

If I was asked to pledge a sorority, I still hoped it would be the Thetas. But although I preferred them, there were a couple of other clubs I liked almost as well. At least, I didn't have my heart set on just one, the way Marilyn did. I couldn't help worrying a little about her and I knew Suz felt the same. But all any of us could do now was wait and see.

I didn't get too much out of my classes that first day. My teachers seemed as if they were going to be all right and I found out where the various classrooms were and picked up my assignments for the next day and met a few of my fellow students. There was an undercurrent of excitement running strong just beneath the surface, but I guess the professors must have known how it always was the first day, before the pledge bids were received. And they made allowances.

I hurried back to Mercer when my final class was over. The sorority bids, all in big square white envelopes, were on a table in the hall. A crowd of girls were gathered around, more quiet than usual and looking a bit strained, picking out the bids addressed to them. I found two with my name on them and my heart thumped heavily as I stood back a little to open them. The first bid was from the Taus, Alicia's influence, I suspected, and my throat ached with disappointment. Then I managed to run an unsteady finger under the flap of the second envelope. The Theta crest leaped at me from the top of the folded sheet, even before I had a chance to read the words beneath it. I felt my lips curve into a smile and happiness exploded in me, so that I wanted to jump up and down and shout. But I restrained the impulse.

I looked around and saw that some of the girls milling about seemed happy and some disappointed. A few looked positively stricken and I dropped my own gaze from the stark hurt in their eyes. Why should I be so lucky, I wondered, when some others—

Suddenly I thought of Marilyn and my own pleasure dimmed a bit. What had happened to her, I wondered? She was nowhere in sight and when I asked if anyone had seen her, Patsy said she thought she'd picked up a bid and then gone up to her room.

It didn't sound good. I ran up the stairs quickly, apprehension growing in me. When I pushed open the door of our room, I saw Marilyn standing at the dresser, stuffing things blindly into her suitcase, tears streaming down her face. The sound of her crying was harshly audible and I pushed the door shut behind me and hurried over to put my arm around her shaking shoulders.

"Marilyn, honey, don't—" I began.

But she pulled away from me and bent her head lower over her packing. "Leave me alone," she gulped. "I'm going home—I hate it here—" Her voice broke.

I stood there, wondering what to say, what to do. But I knew I must say something, so I started talking. "The Taus didn't ask you. But is that any reason to quit school?" I shoved my own bid from them, the one I didn't intend to accept, far down in my skirt pocket. There was no reason to let her know about that. "There are other sororities. You got a bid from one of them, didn't you?"

She drew in a long, quivering breath and motioned disdainfully toward the waste basket. "The Thetas," she said, "but they can have their old bid—if I can't join Tau Kappa I don't want any second-b-best!"

"I got a Theta bid, too," I told her, fishing the crumpled white sheet she had discarded out of the basket and smoothing it under my fingers. "Of course, it's different with me. They're the ones I want to join. But even if none of the clubs had asked me to pledge, I'd have stayed on here. After all, college is a lot more important than any sorority. Where's your perspective?"

She turned a piteous tear-streaked face toward me and her fingers slowed down a little with her haphazard packing, or at least, I hoped they did. "I was so sure they'd ask me," she whispered. "They seemed to like me and I tried so hard—" her voice trailed off again.

She had tried hard, I thought, maybe too hard. Or any number of angles might have entered into it, just as Alicia had explained when I asked her about Hash

Sessions. Maybe the Taus needed brainy types this year, to bring up their scholastic average, instead of Beauty Queen possibilities, such as Marilyn well might be. Or maybe they had too many legacies. Or maybe someone had thought she seemed too anxious.

"How do you know you'd like being a Tau better than a Theta?" I heard my voice asking. I went on, talking soothingly, trying to get her straightened out so that she could look at things less emotionally, so that her common sense, if she had any, would begin to start functioning.

Suz came in while I was working on her and she joined forces with me. Both of us hovered over Marilyn like a couple of anxious mother hens with one contrary little chick, pointing out the merits of the Thetas, overemphasizing the drawbacks of the Taus. We cajoled and argued and gradually Marilyn stopped crying and began to get mad at the Taus for not asking her to join them. This both Suz and I took as a healthy change of attitude. And we encouraged it.

By dinnertime, Marilyn still hadn't entirely given up the idea of leaving Central and going home, but Suz and I had persuaded her to sleep on it, at least. And surely, by morning, she'd be able to see the absurdity of her actions.

Her face still looked a little puffy and her eyes somewhat pink when we all went down to the dining room. But there were others in the same situation, so that no one paid any attention. Those of us who had been asked to pledge the sorority we preferred kept a tight rein on our pleasure, so as not to rub it in on those who had fared less well. Or, at least, we tried to.

Suz leaned across the table to tell me, "I'm going to

miss you, Tobey. If you were staying on at Mercer, there's no one I'd rather have for a roommate."

I felt exactly the same way. "It's been fun, hasn't it? But we aren't going to stop being friends, you dope, just because I'll be staying at the Theta House."

"It'll be different, though," Suz said, a little note of regret in her voice. "After all, we won't be living under the same roof any more."

"We'll be on the same campus, though," I reminded her. "And after all, Central's not such a big college we can't keep in touch."

"Of course not," Suz agreed in a sort of we'll-wait-and-see tone.

But I had no doubt of our continuing friendship. My being a Theta wasn't going to affect that.

Accidents Will Happen

As SUZ AND I HAD HOPED, MARILYN'S BETTER JUDGMENT
took over sometime during the night and she decided to
stay at Central and be pledged to the Thetas after all. I
can't say she seemed very happy about it, but she was resigned. Liking the Thetas so well, I resented her attitude
a little. But I figured that when Marilyn knew them
better she'd be more enthusiastic and less martyred.

On Friday Mercer Hall lost a lot of its Rush Week
residents. Several of us moved over to the Theta house.
It developed that Marilyn and I were going to be roommates, a circumstance that didn't exactly overjoy me, although I managed to conceal my inner feelings. True
to form, Marilyn started out by complaining privately,
but bitterly, to me about practically everything. She
considered the size of our room and particularly the
closet space inadequate. She didn't like the pink and
gray color scheme. She took as a personal affront the
fact that we were half a hall-length from the bath and
shower room. None of these things bothered me in the
slightest degree and this Marilyn couldn't understand.

"We simply look at things differently," I tried to explain. "I like our room, I think it's cozy. And if we use

a little organization, we'll get by fine with the closet space."

Marilyn sighed. "You certainly are easy to suit," she accused. "But then, this was the sorority you wanted, wasn't it?"

"It was and is," I said firmly as I began hanging my clothes up in my half of the closet.

That night the Thetas had an informal pledging party for us newcomers, with a wonderfully festive dinner in the big, high-ceilinged dining-room. There was one small mishap. A freshman student waiter dropped a tray of dishes with a tremendous disrupting clamor just as the chapter president arose to make her welcoming speech. I couldn't help feeling sorry for the poor guy, who blushed with embarrassment all the way up from his white jacket to his stubby blond hair.

"Think nothing of it," Geri Clair leaned across the table to whisper to me laughingly. "It always takes a few days for the new waiters to hit their stride. After that, it's quieter."

When the mess had been cleared away, Rhonda Carter, the president, went on with her little talk. She introduced the other officers of the sorority and our housemother, Mrs. Penn, plumply pleasant, with white hair framing a youthful face. Rhonda went on then to explain that until we were initiated into full membership, we would have to do all the pledge duties assigned to us. These would consist of some menial tasks, such as polishing silver and keeping the plants watered, as well as carrying out any order given us by the actives.

"But you won't find us too hard on you," Rhonda promised with her winning smile. "After all, we like you, or we wouldn't have asked you to pledge."

When she had finished, there were some sorority songs and then came the ceremony of pinning a pledge ribbon of rose and green, the Theta colors, on each of us thrilled newcomers. The little knot of silken ribbon pinned to my dress made me feel proud and happy. It was going to be fun to be a Theta. I felt more sure than ever of that now.

The next day being Saturday, we pledges had to get up early and go down to the kitchen to help fix breakfast for the regular members, then serve it in bed to those who wanted it that way. Marilyn was indignant at the whole idea.

"You wouldn't have thought a thing of it, if it were the Taus," I pointed out to her as we were dressing.

"Maybe not," Marilyn admitted grumpily. "But I'm not going to let them treat me like a servant around here. I won't put up with it!"

"It's only a gag this first day," I told her. "Where's your sense of humor?"

I knew by this time that Marilyn wasn't blessed with much humor. Still, I didn't want her getting off on the wrong foot in the sorority right at the start if I could possibly kid her out of it.

Down in the big, sunny kitchen, with the fragrance of coffee and bacon pleasant on the air, we joined several other yawning pledges and had our first encounter with the cook, Mrs. Knippen.

"The K in my name is silent as in knife and everyone calls me Nippy, so you pledges might as well get into the habit early," the round-cheeked, roly-poly little brunette explained to us. She had a warm, wide smile and a bouncy sort of energy that made her nickname seem singularly appropriate. She kept up a running, bubbling comment as she transferred bacon and eggs to plates and showed us where the orange juice was kept so we could fill the glasses. "This breakfast in bed stuff is just a sort of baptism by fire the actives give you. If you're good-natured about it, the whole idea will blow over in a day or so. It always has before. Of course, if you carry a chip on your shoulder, it makes the whole business more fun and they might keep it up. Just don't say I didn't warn you."

I liked Nippy at once. And I hoped Marilyn was taking in the sound advice the cook was giving her. But her face remained closed and unresponsive as she regarded the breakfast trays on the big table. Why did she have to be like that, I wondered?

Our pledge duties were over for the morning by ten o'clock. As I went through the wide front hall on my way toward the stairs and my room, I saw the mail lying in a flat basket on the table. And right on top was a letter from Brose. My heart skipped a couple of beats as I reached for it. I'd been almost too busy the past week to realize that all I'd had from Brose so far was a long silence. But now and then the realization had thrust itself upon me and I'd thought fleetingly, The stinker! Still, I supposed he'd been busy, too. I'd only written him once, but that had been a long, newsy letter, filled with all the things I'd been doing and admitting frankly that I missed him. Seeing his big scrawly handwriting made me more sharply aware than ever of how much I'd missed him.

I took the curving stairs quickly, hoping that Marilyn wouldn't be back in our room yet, anxious to have a few minutes all to myself with Brose's first letter. Luck was with me, she wasn't there. I flopped down on my tummy across the foot of my bed, opened the envelope and slid out the single sheet of paper.

There were exactly six lines on it, counting the "Dear Tobey:" as one and the "Love, Brose" as another. He had written: "Boy, are they keeping us busy—placement tests, rushing, all the stuff you're going through. Got all my subjects lined up. Looks like I'll have a lot of studying. I pledged Sigma Gamma. More next time. I miss you."

I lay there, staring at the letter disappointedly. The meager words didn't even sound like Brose, not the Brose I knew. Couldn't he squeeze in time to write a little more fully? Then another thought struck me. Was he one of those people who froze up when he started putting his thoughts on paper? Our friendship had always been on a person-to-person basis. We lived only a few blocks apart, had gone to the same school. Our families even spent their vacations at the same lake, so we'd never been separated for any length of time. Brose might always have been a miserable letter writer, stiff and inarticulate, and I just wouldn't have any chance to know it. Now that I thought about it, I remembered how much trouble he'd had with English themes and other written work at school. Why, I asked myself unhappily, hadn't I realized before that our correspondence might not work out too well?

I read his letter over again. It still said practically nothing in as few words as possible. But, at least, he had written that he missed me. I tried to concentrate on that and forget my disappointment. Maybe, I hoped, when he'd had a little more practice, his letters would improve. . . .

After lunch I did some studying. College assignments,

I had already learned, were tougher than those given
you in high school. I doubted that I could get by with
as little homework as I used to do. And the Thetas had
made it very clear to us pledges that they expected us
to keep our grades up. Even without this additional
prod, I would have wanted to do as well as I could at
college. It seemed to me that when one's parents went
to all the expense of paying one's way through school,
the least they could expect was some co-operation. Not
that I intended to turn into a Grind. I hadn't the
temperament for that. But enough studying to maintain
a B average shouldn't tax me so much that I couldn't
have a well-rounded social life, too. And I knew that
would keep my parents satisfied and happy.

Marilyn joined me in our room and did some studying, too, although she stopped quite frequently to complain about the amount of homework our teachers had
loaded us down with.

"If you'd concentrate more and gripe less," I finally
said, more truthfully than tactfully, "you'd get done
faster."

Marilyn gave me a dirty look, but she quit interrupting
me every five minutes, so it was worth it. We both
leaned back half an hour later, almost at the same instant,
and shut our books.

"Finished?" I asked. Then, as she nodded, I suggested, "Let's walk over to the Barn and have a soda.
We can phone Suz and see if she can't meet us there."

"Why get Suz?" Marilyn inquired, going over to the
dressing table to freshen her lipstick.

Our eyes met in the mirror as I said firmly, "Because
I like Suz. And I'd like to see her." I frowned then,

demanding, "Or do you only intend to associate with sorority members from now on?"

"Don't be silly," Marilyn said. But the slight flush that reddened her cheeks made me suspect that my half-kidding remark had come rather close to the truth.

As it worked out, Suz wasn't in when I called Mercer Hall a few minutes later. So Marilyn and I went without her to the Barn, after all. This was an old red frame building that had actually been a barn at one time and was now the favorite campus hangout for sodas and malts. It had a long old-fashioned counter with decrepit stools along one side and a row of booths at the other. Every booth was occupied with laughing, animated four-somes or sixsomes, or quiet, dreamy-eyed twosomes. But Marilyn and I found a couple of vacant stools at one end of the fountain and gave our orders.

The atmosphere of the place reminded me a little of Joe's Grill back in Edgewood. But if this had been Joe's, I'd have been surrounded by familiar faces instead of people I didn't know. And Brose would most likely have been with me. At the thought I felt a miserable un-happy twinge.

"Do you see anyone you know?" Marilyn asked wist-fully.

I shook my head. "Not a soul." Then I added, try-ing to sound more cheerful. "It won't be like this long, though. We'll get acquainted with lots of people pretty soon. It just takes a little while. Why, by this time next week, we'll probably see several people we know, if we come in here."

"I hope so." Marilyn sighed. "When I think of this being Saturday, tonight being Saturday night and not hav-ing a date—" her voice sort of trailed off.

"Yeah," I agreed.

The counter man, who was middle-aged and looked as though he had seen too many college students to tell one from another, set our sodas down before us and marked the check. They were tasty enough sodas, complete with whipped cream and cherries on top, but my appetite didn't seem as good as usual. I guessed I was a little homesick just then. I think Marilyn was, too. We went on, sipping our sodas and not saying much.

When we had finished, I suggested, "Let's go back to the House. At least there we'll see some friends."

We scuffed along through the golden fallen leaves that were drifting across the campus. The wind was cool with a touch of drizzle edging it. I pulled the collar of my jacket closer around my neck and walked faster.

Marilyn said plaintively, "According to the catalogue Central sent me when I was trying to decide on a college, there are a hundred or so more male students here than female."

I nodded. "Wonder where they're hiding?"

We both laughed then and I began to feel a little better. I assured Marilyn staunchly as we turned toward the Theta House, "Don't worry. They'll be eating out of our hands as soon as we've had time to get acquainted with a few of them."

"Sure," Marilyn agreed. "It's just that it seems so queer not to have a date on Saturday night."

It did, indeed. The evening stretched ahead, almost frightening in its emptiness. I supposed I could spend a part of it answering Brose's letter. Or there might be a good movie at one of the two local shows. Maybe some of the other Thetas would be planning to go. A hen party would be better than none at all.

I took a shower before dinner and did my nails and put on my blue jersey dress with the gold belt. I'd read somewhere that looking your best gave your morale a boost. Besides, it was a Theta custom to dress up a bit for dinner. Marilyn showered and changed her clothes, too. When the gong sounded we went downstairs together and found our places.

A couple of the pledges had dates for the evening, but most were in the same boat with Marilyn and me.

"How did you work so fast?" I asked one of the lucky ones. "I hardly know any men yet!"

"It was easy," Jean Clyde, a perky brunette, confided. "I just came to the same college my favorite guy picked."

Why hadn't I gone West with Brose, or persuaded him to come to Central with me, I asked myself morosely? Still, I knew in my heart that wouldn't have been a good idea. If neither of us had a chance to date other people, how would we ever know whether the way we felt about each other was real, or just a habit? This way was best, even though I did feel lonely and left out at first. It wouldn't always be like this.

The sound of clattering dishes yanked me abruptly out of my reverie. But before I could grasp what was happening, disaster had struck. The contents of a whole tray of salads came cascading down my back in a shower of fruit and cottage cheese and mayonnaise dressing.

I let out a shrill little yelp of dismay and stared up into the appalled, slowly reddening face of the same clumsy young man who had dumped a tray of dishes on the floor during our pledge dinner.

seven

Dave

"I WILL NEVER FORGET," DAVE JOHNSEN INFORMED ME, "how accusing your face looked as you turned around with cottage cheese dripping down your neck."

It was an hour after the accident and Dave and I were walking across the campus through the drizzly rain on our way to the Barn. Which just goes to show, you never can tell how an evening will turn out.

"Well, you didn't really think I'd be pleased, did you?" I couldn't resist asking.

"No." Dave grinned. His grin was so appealing, his whole personality so engaging, I hadn't been able to stay mad at him very long. He had apologized for the mishap with such sincerity. And he had rushed out to the kitchen for a dampened towel and tried to dab away the mess he had made. So what could I do but say it was all right and tell him to forget it?

But he had waylaid me at the door when I'd started upstairs to change my dress and had begged me to have a Coke with him when he went off duty, just to prove I'd forgiven him. And I'd said okay, because that seemed the natural thing to say under the circumstances. And now here we were, heading for the Barn and talking as easily to each other as though we were old friends.

Dave had shed his white waiter's coat in favor of a rather shapeless tweed sport jacket. His blond head, with the very short haircut, was bare. His hands were shoved deep into the pockets of his slacks as we strolled along and his shoulders were hunched a little against the rain. He was only a couple of inches taller than I, so that our eyes were almost on a level as we looked at each other and talked. Never had I met anyone who was easier to talk with.

Before we had got off the Theta House porch, he had told me that his name was Dave Johnsen and had explained that it was spelled with an e instead of an o. "That's because I'm Danish descent, not Swedish," he had informed me. "The Danes end their names with 'sen,' as in Hans Christian Andersen. You can always tell the difference that way. My grandfather was born in Denmark," he had gone on, "not far from Elsinore Castle."

"You mean Elsinore's a real place?" I had asked, surprised. I'd always supposed it was just a setting Shakespeare had made up for Hamlet.

"Sure, it is," Dave had said. "Of course, it's a ruin. Grandpop has a painting of it he made when he was around my age."

"Is he an artist?" I asked.

Dave gave a chortle of laughter. "Grandpop? He's a carpenter. He only paints as a hobby, but he's not bad for an amateur. Hey!" he exclaimed. "How did we get on the subject of my grandfather before you've even told me your name?"

So I told him. And then he made the remark about how appalled I'd looked when he spilled the salads on me. Which led, naturally, to his telling me about how being a waiter was hard at first, till you got the hang of it. And that led to his explaining that he was working his way through college.

"It's the only way I could get here," he said. "I'm the oldest in a family of five kids. And shoes for the younger ones are more vital than higher learning for the older— that is, unless I can earn it for myself. This is a good school for fellows like me. Quite an extensive work program and enough of us are taking advantage of it so that there's no social stigma attached. Not," he added, "that it would bother me if there was, you understand."

"No disgrace in working," I said.

"My sentiments exactly," Dave agreed.

We had reached the Barn by that time and he held the door open for me politely. We found a corner booth and Dave got us each a Coke from the fountain and brought them over. "I hope this is okay," he said. "It's pretty soon after dinner for a hamburger or anything— and besides, I'm broke."

"This is fine," I told him. He certainly was a young man without pretenses. And I liked his frankness, his utter lack of phoniness or affectation.

Dave sat down opposite me and sloshed the cracked ice in his drink around and around. "The only trouble is, between my studies and working, I don't have much free time. Would you believe it," he inquired, "this is the first Coke I've had with a girl since school started."

It was the first one I'd had with a boy, too, but not because I lacked the time. I didn't say so, though. Instead, I reminded him, "That hasn't been very long— only ten days."

"Yeah, but I wouldn't be doing it now," Dave explained seriously, "if it hadn't been for what I did to you back there at the sorority house and wanting to make amends and all." He grinned then, and demanded, "You know what? I'm kind of glad it happened. Well—not really, because of your having to get your dress cleaned, but—you know how I mean?"

I thought I did. I couldn't help smiling back at him.

"Sure you do," Dave said. "It would probably have been months before I'd have been able to get acquainted with any of you girls, if it hadn't been for the accident tonight. That is, there are so many of you and a guy can't just go up to a girl at random and say 'how about having a soda with me?' He'd feel he had to ask her on a real date, a movie or even a dance or something. And I haven't got that kind of money."

"I can pay for my own Coke," I teased, sipping it.

"You don't have to do that," Dave said. "Not this time. I just figured I ought to make my position clear right off, so there'd be no room for misunderstanding. I'm really broke. And I expect to go on being broke all the time I'm in college. I've got three jobs, but it takes all I can earn from them just to keep abreast of my expenses."

"Three jobs?" I stared at him. "What are the other two?"

"I'm janitor at the Zeta Mu fraternity house. I'm a pledge technically, but I do janitoring to pay my living expenses and earn some extra money besides. And I work in the library on Saturdays."

"Doesn't leave you much spare time, does it?" I smiled at him. "Which job are you a fugitive from right now?"

"Ummm, none exactly," Dave told me. "I'll have to

get back to the Zeta house before long and walk Baby. That's always my final duty for the day."

"Baby?" I repeated faintly.

"Our mascot. Surely you've seen Baby around the campus."

"You mean that enormous St. Bernard dog?"

"Sure." Dave beamed. "That's Baby. Say," he exclaimed, apparently struck by a sudden idea, "I don't suppose you'd want to walk with me when I take her out?"

I thought a moment. Of course, it was drizzling a little, but I was wearing my raincoat. And I'd always sort of liked to walk in the rain. Dave was such fun to talk to, I wasn't averse to spending some more time in his company. I couldn't see what I had to lose.

"Why not?" I asked with a little shrug.

"Say!" Dave exclaimed. "You are a good scout, spending this much time with a guy who hasn't any money to take you any place special."

"What did you think I was," I asked, pushing my empty glass aside, "a gold digger?"

"Well, no." Dave finished his drink, too. "But my impression of most college girls, especially sorority girls, is that they don't want to waste time on a guy unless he's got money to spend."

"A hasty generalization," I said, "if I ever heard one. And just as false as most hasty generalizations are."

"Maybe you're right at that," Dave admitted.

"How many sorority girls have you known well enough to figure you can tell exactly what they think?" I pressed my point further. "The Thetas are certainly a friendly, unpretentious bunch with too much sense just to be willing to date heavy spenders."

"Yeah, they do seem that way," Dave said, "especially the one I've had the most conversation with—you." He fished a couple of coins out of his pocket to pay for our drinks. "Come on, let's go walk Baby."

The rain had practically stopped when we got outside. There was a flying wrack of clouds overhead, moving as fast as clipper ships across the sky. But the wind was warmer and there was such a moist freshness in the air it had the feel of spring. We talked on half a dozen subjects as we crossed the campus toward Dave's fraternity house. He wasn't a person you could ever run out of conversation with. He was interested in everything. And he seemed to know quite a lot about every topic that came up, not in a show-off-ish way, but as though his natural intellectual curiosity was so great it had led him to explore a variety of subjects. He was a science major, but when he learned that I was majoring in education, with the intention of teaching English, we launched into a lively discussion of that. And it turned out that Dave had been editor of his high school paper and had been undecided for a while as to whether to concentrate on English or science.

"What made you decide on science?" I asked.

"A teacher I had in high school," Dave admitted. "Maybe it sounds corny to say he inspired me, but that comes the closest to describing it of any word I know."

"Sometimes," I told him, "I think our generation is too scared of sounding corny. If we lean too much the other way, we're in danger of being cynical and materialistic. And that's worse than corny." I sounded so serious I got a little embarrassed, although I meant exactly what I said.

"I think you're right," Dave agreed. He didn't seem

at all amused at my outburst and I liked him even better for it.

"What was your science teacher like?" I asked.

I could make out Dave's grin in the darkness. "Just himself," he said. "Nobody else in the wide world. A kind of thin old guy, must be close to retirement age, only if the school board ever retires him, it's crazy. You keep reading how the country's supply of scientists isn't what it should be and how young people should be urged into studying science. He never urges anybody. All he does is make the subject so fascinating, most of the kids he teaches decide to go to college and major in it. Our high school back home isn't one of your great big modern educational institutions. And Doc Thurston's lab leaves a lot to be desired when it comes to new equipment. But that doesn't stop Doc. When something breaks down he just patches it up and keeps on going. Sometimes the students repair the broken-down equipment and learn a lot by doing it. Besides that, he gets your curiosity aroused, gets you wondering about things, so that you've just got to go on studying to learn more about it all."

"He sounds like quite a person," I said.

By that time we had reached the Zeta House, a mid-Victorian mansion that had seen better days, but still managed to retain a sort of gingerbready, be-cupola-ed charm. I waited outside while Dave went in and got Baby. The two of them came galumphing down the walk a couple of minutes later, Dave attached to the other end of Baby's thick chain leash, as though she were taking him for a walk instead of vice versa. She was a beautiful dog in a monsterish sort of way, her hair brown and white and silky, her tail a sweeping plume. She greeted me affectionately, if a little overwhelmingly, her great wet tongue slobbering over my hands which I'd stretched out to ward off her caress. Luckily I was wearing my raincoat, because Baby was not to be warded off.

"She likes you," Dave informed me, as though the news should make me very happy.

"She's got my whole hand in her mouth," I objected faintly.

"That's a sure sign she likes you," he said. "She won't really bite. I've never seen her more friendly than this with anyone."

"I should hope not," I murmured. "Any more friendly and she'd probably eat me up."

"Don't worry," Dave counseled. "She's just a pup. When she gets older she'll be calm and quiet. The brothers are starting in training her now, but it'll take time."

Baby decided at this point to get on with the business at hand, namely, to go for a walk. She pulled Dave along behind her and I had to hurry to keep up. We circled the campus a couple of times and explored two or three side streets at such a fast pace I was out of breath and so was Dave, I guessed, because our conversation sort of languished.

But when we had taken Baby back to the fraternity house once more and Dave came out to walk me home, we started talking again and it was just as interesting as before.

"This has been fun," Dave told me at the front door of the Theta House. "We'll have to do it again—that is, if you enjoyed it, too." His tone held a question.

"I did." I smiled up at him. "I had a lot of fun. I may even get used to Baby in time."

"Sure you will," Dave said, giving my elbow a friendly little squeeze in farewell. " 'Bye, now."

He loped off into the darkness and I went into the house and shut the door behind me. Some of the pledges had a couple of tables of bridge under way in the lounge off the front hall and I went in for a minute to watch.

Marilyn happened to be dummy and she looked up at me, her brown eyes frankly envious. "Hi, lucky," she said.

"Lucky?"

"You had a date, didn't you?" Marilyn queried.

"Well—" I hesitated, smiling, "I guess so. I had a Coke and went for a walk with a boy, if you call that a date."

"Was that all?" Marilyn asked. "I thought at least he'd take you to the movies."

"I think he's cute," Marilyn's partner remarked, as she picked up the final trick. "He's pretty clumsy when it comes to waiting table, but I imagine he's fun."

"Oh, he is that," I agreed. "Very interesting."

If this was a date I'd just had, though, it certainly was one of the least conventional ones I could imagine. But there was no getting around the fact that I'd enjoyed myself. Had Dave really had fun, too, enough so that he might ask me to have a Coke another time and go for another walk with him and Baby? He'd implied that he had and would—but you never could tell about boys.

eight

Mysterious Phone Call

I SAW LITTLE OF DAVE JOHNSEN THE NEXT WEEK, EXCEPT in the dining room when he was intent on his duties, and on a couple of very brief occasions when Baby got away from the Zeta house and came over to see me. It seemed that Baby had developed a mad passion for my company and, whenever she got out loose, she made a beeline for the Theta House. Once she got all the way inside and sniffed her unerring way up the stairs to my room, followed by little yelps of amazement and dismay as startled Thetas scattered in all directions. I had to admit that Baby was rather a disconcerting sight, all one hundred and sixty-five pounds of her, as she launched herself joyously at me. But I managed to calm her down and a couple of minutes later Dave's anxious voice was heard in the downstairs hall, calling Baby's name and whistling beguilingly. All Baby did was cock her great head curiously and continue to hold my hand wetly and affectionately in her mouth.

"It just means she likes me," I assured Marilyn, who had taken refuge behind her bed. "She isn't really biting."

"Well, get her out of here," Marilyn commanded shrilly. "She scares me, she's so big."

Baby and I went, hand in mouth, out into the hall and down the stairs. At sight of Dave, she let my hand go and rushed delightedly toward him. When he had managed to snap on her leash, he breathed a sigh of relief. "What is this power you have over dogs?" he asked me, grinning. "She's crazy about you."

"I love her, too," I laughed. "But I'm afraid most of my sorority sisters don't share my enthusiasm."

"I'll try to keep her away," Dave called back over his shoulder as he and Baby left. "I'm sorry she gave you trouble."

Not a word about seeing me again. I couldn't help wondering whether it was because he was too broke, or too busy, or whether he simply wasn't interested. I sighed a little disappointed sigh as the door closed after him.

My days were so filled with classes and my evenings with studying that I didn't have much time to brood over Dave Johnsen. We were kept hopping with pledge duties, too, around the sorority house. Pledge, do this! Hey, pledge, take care of that, will you? It was a fairly constant chorus in our ears. I didn't really mind, though. The Thetas weren't too rough on us. And they were almost always agreeable and friendly, which made for pleasant relationships all around.

I thought that Marilyn was getting a little better adjusted as the days marched past. She didn't seem to complain as much, or could it be that I was becoming so accustomed to her griping that I didn't really hear it? We got along fairly well, although there were other pledges I felt I'd have been happier rooming with.

Suz Herrick and I were in the same English Comp class, so I saw her every day. We usually walked together afterward, until our paths toward our next classes separated. I still liked Suz best of all the girls I'd met since coming to college. When I told her about Dave Johnsen, Suz said, "He sounds like quite a guy. I'd like to meet him."

"I wouldn't mind spending some more time with him myself," I admitted ruefully. "But I don't know if I'll have a chance."

"Why not?" Suz queried. "He certainly sounds interested."

"But he hasn't any money," I reminded, "and practically no spare time. That combination doesn't make for a very active social life, I'm afraid."

I didn't really have my heart set on Dave Johnsen, although I'd enjoyed the time I'd spent with him. All I actually wanted was a date. And the fact that I hadn't had a real one since coming to college was the reason I was feeling a bit left out and neglected. Oh, I'd met quite a lot of boys in class and through sorority sisters and other acquaintances. And these were friendly enough when it came to a casual encounter on campus or at the Barn. But a date was something else.

I indulged in a pleasant little day-dream about how some evening just as I was leaving the dining room, the phone would ring and whoever answered it would sing out, "Man on the wire for Tobey." In my dream I wasn't at all sure who this man might be. It really didn't make much difference, unless he was someone absolutely repulsive. Just so long as he had something interesting to suggest, like a small informal party at his fraternity house, or a movie, or even, if it should happen to be Dave, a walk with him and Baby. I'd settle for almost anything, I was getting that desperate!

I couldn't remember when I'd gone two whole weeks without a date before. And it didn't help matters any that I hadn't heard from Brose since that first short unsatisfactory letter. I was sorry now that I'd answered it so promptly. Still, annoyed as I was with him, I looked anxiously through the mail every day. But all I ever got was a letter from home, or from Barbie. And she seemed just a little like a stranger to me since she had decided to call herself Lynn.

Of course, there were lots of other girls who hadn't had any dates, either. Marilyn, however, had managed to get out of her slump. She was so pretty that this wasn't particularly surprising. Still, I'd never considered myself completely unattractive. I supposed it just took time to meet the right men who would prove susceptible to my charms. At least, I hoped so.

There was going to be a big Freshman Mixer in the gym on Friday night and I was secretly pinning my hopes on that to break the ice and really start things rolling for me. It didn't help my morale to discover that my roommate was going to it with a boy she'd met in biology class, while I would just be accompanied by a couple of other pledges.

"Why didn't you tell me sooner?" Marilyn asked as we were dressing that night. "Maybe Bill could have got someone for you."

Her condescending attitude made me see slightly red, but I controlled my temper and said merely, "Oh, I'd rather go with Carol and Evelyn. Blind dates never appealed to me. This way we can look over all the available males and see which ones we want to encourage."

"If," Marilyn said cattily, "there are enough males to go around."

She must have been psychic—there weren't! The Mixer committee did its best to keep the shortage from spoiling things. Ladies' Choice dances and a Conga Line helped some. Dave wasn't there. Probably he was working at one of his various jobs. A couple of the men I'd met in class asked me to dance, for which I felt abjectly grateful. Several times I glimpsed Marilyn across the big, brightly decorated room, dancing with the tall, dark and flatteringly attentive man who had brought her. I almost regretted I hadn't thrown myself on her mercy in time for her to fix me up with a blind date. Never in my life had I come so sickeningly close to being a wallflower.

I was inwardly relieved when it was late enough so that Carol and Evelyn and I could leave, without it looking like a retreat. Probably they felt the same way, but none of us would admit it. We walked back to the Theta House across the starlit campus, arm in arm, but not talking very much. There didn't seem to be a great deal to say.

I ran into Suz Saturday morning in the library. Dave was at the desk and I introduced Suz and him. After a couple of minutes of casual friendly conversation, I told Dave, "I didn't see you at the Mixer last night."

"I was there," he said. "You just didn't look in the right place. I was playing the bass viol in the combo."

"You were?" I asked in astonishment. I hadn't looked at the orchestra very closely, though, and a bass viol is a pretty formidable instrument to see over. "I didn't know you were a musician."

"Well—" said Dave with a chuckle, "if you use the

term loosely." He said then, "I felt obligated to earn
the ten bucks I was paid for the evening, or I'd have
skipped a number and asked you to dance. But I'm
the conscientious type, darn it."

Suz and I laughed and, a few minutes later, strolled
out into the crisp autumn sunshine. The sky was clear
and blue and a scent of leaf smoke hung hauntingly on
the air.

"I like your friend Dave," Suz said.

I nodded. "He's cute." Then I smiled faintly, remembering what he'd said, "But I'm not sure he's my
friend, letting money come between us like that." A
thought struck me suddenly and I asked, "Why weren't
you at the Mixer, Suz?"

She smiled, shaking her head. "Affairs like that always
turn out to involve dancing. And men never pay the
slightest attention to me. Not that I care especially,
but after a while I begin to feel conspicuous—so I just
don't go."

"They didn't pay much attention to me, either." It
was so easy to tell the truth to Suz. "Two of them asked
me to dance during the whole evening."

"Two would be a good number for me," Suz said
philosophically. "But you're so attractive, I'm astonished.
The fellows around here mustn't have good eyesight, or
something."

My ego perked up a bit under her kind words. What
a pal she was. But I said, "No reason they should go
for me more than you."

Suz chuckled. "Let's face it. I'll probably develop
into a reasonably attractive woman as I grow older. I
may marry a worthwhile man and have a happy, stimulating life and scads of darling children. But right now,

at eighteen, I'm not what is known as 'date bait'—but you are. It may take a few weeks for you to hit your stride here at college, but you'll hit it. And that, my child, is old Granny Herrick's prediction for the day," she finished in a quavering falsetto. Then, laughing, we linked arms and headed for the Barn and a soda to tide us over till lunchtime.

I felt a twinge of sympathy for Suz. But she seemed so unconcerned about her failure to attract boys that I guessed it didn't really bother her. As for me, my spirits had risen considerably. Suz's staunch assurance that my college life was sure to pick up soon gave me a badly needed shot of self-confidence.

But, as is the way with shots, the effect soon began to wear off. I couldn't seem to forget that it was Saturday again and once more I was dateless. I worked my way doggedly through my pledge duties, which seemed more boring than usual. I did all my homework, even finishing a book report for English which wouldn't be due until Tuesday. I went in to town shopping and bought tooth paste and nail polish and stationery, in case I was reduced to spending the evening writing letters. I checked both theaters hopefully, but one had a war picture and I hated war pictures. The other was running a musical I'd seen back in Edgewood a month ago.

On my way back to the campus I passed a record shop with a loud-speaker over the door. The tune that came blaring out was one Brose and I had danced to a lot last summer. Memories welled up in me and I hurried on, missing Brose, homesick for my family, so miserable I felt like crying, but determined not to. The sight of the Theta House looming big and friendly through the early dusk pushed back the tears and made my feet hurry faster.

I encountered Geri Clair in the hall and she gave me a wide warm smile. "Hi, Tobey."

"Hi!" My voice sounded higher pitched than usual, it was so determinedly cheerful.

A little questioning look came into Geri's eyes. "Have you been out long—or did you get your phone call?"

"Phone call?" I repeated blankly.

"About half an hour ago," Geri elucidated. "Some guy called you. I heard Jean Clyde trying to find you for him."

"I was out then." I gulped. "Do you know who it was?"

Geri shook her head regretfully. "Ask Jean. Maybe she took a message."

I finally located Jean just coming out of the shower room, draped sarong-fashion in a yellow towel. "Who called me?" I asked anxiously.

"He didn't say," Jean admitted. "But I told him you'd be back by dinnertime and he said he'd try again then."

I hadn't realized I was holding my breath till I heard it puff out in a disappointed sigh. Dinnertime was half an hour away. How could I ever wait that long?

Possibilities kept crowding into my mind. Could it have been Dave, wanting to squander on me some part of the extra money he'd earned at the Mixer last night? Or one of the boys I'd danced with might have been more deeply impressed than I'd realized. It could even be someone I'd met in one of my classes, the tall blond boy who sat behind me in English, or the plump jolly one who always borrowed my eraser in math.

I dressed for dinner with special care, brushing my hair till it shone and choosing one of the sweaters I hadn't yet worn. Whoever it was who had called me might want to go to the first show at the movies. If I were all ready, we could get an earlier start. I wouldn't even mind seeing a war picture, or a musical for the second time. Not if it meant a Real Date.

When the gong sounded, I floated down to the dining room on a bright pink cloud. I had no idea what I ate, but it must have been delicious because I finished every crumb. Even Marilyn's detailed discussion of her date plans had no effect on my appetite.

As we all left the dining room, the phone rang, just as it had been doing in my favorite daydream. Jean, who happened to be nearest, answered it. Then she said, "Just a minute," and handed the phone to me, whispering, "It's he—the same one."

"Hello?" I murmured into the mouthpiece, my voice just the right mingling of casual interest and agreeable anticipation.

"Hi, Tobey." My heart did a nose dive. Unmistakably, it was only my brother-in-law, Adam Wentworth.

"Oh—Adam." My voice cracked a little, forcing itself through the sick disappointment in my throat.

"Say, we were just wondering," Adam went on hopefully, "if you aren't busy tonight if there's any chance of getting you to baby-sit for some friends of ours? We were all going out together and their sitter let them down at the last minute."

nine

Baby Sitter

THE HARTNETTS, GIL AND JINNY AND THEIR TWO-YEAR-OLD
son, Chris, lived right across the hall from Alicia and
Adam. Chris was sound asleep in his crib when I got
there, for which I was grateful, since my experience in
handling young children wasn't too extensive. He looked
perfectly angelic when Jinny and I tiptoed in to take
a peek at him. His blond head lay peacefully on his
little ruffled pillow and his face was upturned, lashes
golden against his cheeks and pink mouth curled in a
half-smile as though his dreams were pleasant.

"He won't give you any trouble I'm sure," Jinny,
whose pony tail was almost as blond as Chris's curls,
assured me. "He sleeps like a log—except that his teeth
have been giving him just a *little* bit of trouble lately.
If he *should* cry, just get him a drink and pat him a little.
That usually does the trick."

Both she and Gil were most appreciative of my coming
to stay with Chris. Their gratitude gave me a nice little
glow. At least it was good to know that I was helping
to make someone's Saturday night an occasion, even if
my own was a miserable flop.

Gil told me, "We've been planning on this movie all

week. It's a kind of celebration, really, for Jinny's birthday. We don't get out together very often on account of Chris. But we thought we were all set for tonight. My brother Larry was going to sit for us. So what happens? The louse calls at five o'clock and says he can't come. He's involved in a dance committee meeting for his fraternity and can't duck it. At least that's what he claims! We were sure sunk till Alicia thought of calling you."

My dear sister had the grace to give me a faintly apologetic look. Oh, well, I thought philosophically, it was nice to know you were needed.

Adam cut short the Hartnetts' thanks with the announcement that they'd better get going if they wanted to make the first show. The four of them departed and silence settled down over the little apartment. It was quite cozy, I thought, looking around. There were books on low shelves under the window and the draperies were gay, if inexpensive. The apartment consisted of a living room, bedroom and a kitchen so tiny you could stand in the middle and reach anything in it. Jinny had told me hospitably that there were soft drinks in the refrigerator and cookies in the jar and to help myself. I just might do that later.

For the time being I curled up on the slip-covered couch, my feet tucked under me, and thought about what a different sort of experience college must be for married students. There was a picture of Gil in navy blues on the desk, his little white cap set at a jaunty angle. So I theorized that he had probably married Jinny while he was still in the service, or right after getting out. He might have had a year of college before he went in, then decided sensibly to finish his education. And Jinny, I suspected, would be the type to back him up and help him stick to that decision. Maybe they were getting help from their families, or Gil might be attending college under the G.I. Bill. The sight of a much-handled budget book lying on the desk and a big piggy bank on the bookshelves gave me the impression that they probably had to do some penny-pinching. And having a baby would keep them out of a lot of the college social life, although I hoped they were able to manage a dance now and then. Somehow, I was beginning to feel a lot closer to Jinny and Gil after sitting here in their little home, figuring things out about them. I was glad now that I'd been able to come and stay with their baby tonight, so that Jinny's birthday celebration hadn't been spoiled.

After a while I started looking around for something to read and found some paper-backed mystery books tucked away between a chemistry textbook and Roget's Thesaurus. I chose one and went back to the couch to read it, detouring past the bedroom for a reassuring peek at Chris. He was still asleep and still covered up, so I felt free to concentrate on my whodunit. When I glanced at the clock again, more than an hour had passed. It was almost nine.

I did some mental calculations, adding the length of time the average movie took and the half hour or so that might be consumed if the Hartnetts and Alicia and Adam stopped for hamburgers or something afterward at the Barn. Say two and a half or three hours all together. And it had been only a little after seven when they left, so they'd probably get home around ten-thirty. By then I could most likely finish my book.

But before I got on with it, I decided I'd go out and get the drink and cookies Jinny had offered me. I had kicked off my loafers, so I padded out to the little kitchen in my stocking feet. But just as I reached to open the refrigerator, someone knocked on the kitchen door and my heart gave a startled jerk. Who could it be, I wondered? Before I could move, the doorknob turned and the door swung inward and I just stood there, one hand still gripping the icebox handle and the other clutching my book. I'm afraid my mouth had dropped open a little in surprise.

A most attractive young man, tall and dark and broad-shouldered in a belted trench coat, beamed at me from the doorway. "Hey, I made it! Aren't you—" his cheerful voice ran down then, leaving his mouth a little open, too, and his dark brows drew together in a frown of astonishment. "I'm sorry," he said. "I thought this was the Hartnetts'—" once more he broke off. "It *is* the Hartnetts' place! I'd recognize that cockeyed wall plaque anywhere. But—where's Jinny and Gil—and who are you?"

At least, I realized, he was a much less terrifying character than the one who had knocked on the heroine's door in the book I was reading. And since he was on a first name basis with the Hartnetts and enough at home to walk into their kitchen with only a preliminary knock, he must be a good friend of theirs.

I smiled, explaining, "They've gone to the movies. I'm taking care of Chris. My name's Tobey Heydon."

"Well, hi." The young man smiled back at me, coming the rest of the way into the kitchen and shutting the door against the chill autumn wind. "I'm Gil's brother, Larry. I told them I just might be able to make it in time for them to go to the second show, but I guess they were afraid to count on it."

"I guess they were." I replied. "It was a sort of celebration for Jinny's birthday, so I don't suppose they wanted to take a chance." Right at the moment, I was glad they had got me to come instead of counting on Larry's making it later. The kitchen was so small that we had to stand quite close together in order to fit into it at all. I hadn't stood so close to a young man since I'd kissed Brose good-bye in the telephone booth back in Edgewood. The thought just brushed the edge of my mind and was wafted away. I had no intention of thinking about Brose at a time like this.

"Mind if I stick around a while now that I'm here?" Larry Hartnett asked.

I shook my head. I'd have minded very much if he'd turned right around and left. "I was just going to have a Coke," I told him.

"Good," Larry said. "I'll join you."

He got out the bottles and opened them while I took some cookies out of Jinny's well-stocked jar and put them on a plate. Then we went back into the living room and sat down.

"What are you reading?" Larry asked. "Nothing educational, I trust."

"A mystery," I held it up for him to see the garish cover. "That's partly why your knock startled me so."

"You did look a little blank," he said. "But then, I suppose I did, too." He stretched his long legs out comfortably and helped himself to a cookie. "You a freshman?" he asked then.

I nodded. "You mean it's that obvious?"

Larry chuckled. "I wouldn't say that. I just deduced it, like Sherlock Holmes. I thought to myself, now what is such a pretty girl doing baby-sitting on a Saturday night? She should be out on a date. And do you know what the only reasonable explanation for this strange phenomenon is, my dear Watson? She must be a freshman. Because the freshman men are just a little bit slow catching on. And the upperclassmen probably haven't had time to discover her yet."

I sat there smiling, feeling my spirits rise by the minute. This was the sort of thing I'd been missing so. The gay, casual talk. The look in a man's eyes that said quite clearly that he liked me, found me attractive, was enjoying my company. "And you, I take it," I said demurely, "are not a freshman?"

"Please, no insults!" Larry spoke in a tone of mock severity. "I am a man who has tasted college life for two whole years and found it good. Hasn't time left its mark on me? Can't you tell?"

I nodded. "That look of having lived desperately," I went along with the gag, my tone hushed and dramatic, "that interesting touch of gray at the temples, that man-of-the-world air—all these things told me you weren't a freshman."

Larry burst out laughing. He lifted his Coke bottle toward me. "A toast," he said, "to our friendship. I have a feeling you're a girl after my own heart."

We touched bottles and drank and I started laughing, too. But then I remembered and said, "We'd better be more quiet. We might wake the baby."

"Not my nephew." Larry shook his head. "He comes from a long line of heavy sleepers. Why, Jinny practically has to pull the bed out from under Gil to get him up in the morning. You should hear her piteous story."

We sat there, laughing and talking nonsense and eating cookies. Larry had me almost hysterical with his account of the dance committee meeting he had just come from and their subtle efforts to get out of doing any work. "We appointed enough subcommittees to take care of two dances." Larry chuckled. "What a bunch of gold bricks!"

Suddenly a prolonged howl interrupted our conversation. "You and your long line of heavy sleepers," I accused Larry as I hurried toward the bedroom.

Chris was standing up in bed crying, looking small and forlorn in his yellow pajamas, a bedraggled Panda under his arm. He looked flushed and when I reached out for him he felt hot. I picked him up and cuddled him, as Jinny had said to do. "Hi, honey. It's all right. Your mommy will be back soon. Want a drink of water?"

Chris wept harder than ever. I told Larry distractedly, "It's probably because I'm a perfect stranger to the poor little guy. He was asleep when I got here."

Larry reached out for the unhappy baby and I handed him over. "Hi, Butch. How about a big smile for Uncle Larry?" Then to me, "Gee, he feels hot. Maybe he had too many covers on."

Chris's heartbroken wailing seemed to be diminishing a bit. He snuggled his head against Larry's neck and clung to him.

"I hope he hasn't got a temperature." I frowned.

"It's probably teeth," Larry said sagely. "Jinny says cutting teeth affects babies in lots of queer ways." He turned his attention to Chris once more, saying, "You're just nuts, pal, hanging onto me like this when you could be snuggling up to a pretty girl instead. Your father and I are just going to have to explain a few things to you, young man."

Chris stared at me fixedly for a minute. Then he smiled and reached out his arms toward me. I took him from Larry and snuggled him close and he gave me a rather wet kiss full on the mouth. He was really a darling.

"That's better," Larry said. "Now you're getting the idea."

"Don't you suppose we should get him back to bed—" I began. But with that Chris started howling again.

I was a little relieved to hear the living-room door opening and the voices of the Hartnetts and Alicia and Adam.

"He just woke up," I told Jinny apologetically as she came in and Chris went like a little homing pigeon straight into her outstretched arms. "He feels awfully hot."

"It's those molars." Jinny smiled reassuringly at me. "He always runs a temp with teeth."

"Didn't I tell you?" Larry wagged his head.

"You rat," Gil said good-humoredly as Larry and I backed out into the living room, leaving Jinny to minister to her child. "When did you turn up?"

"I told you I'd try to make it later," Larry said.

"Yeah, but I've had too much experience with those 'laters' of yours," Gil said, "to depend on them."

We all stood talking for a few minutes. Then Adam said, "We'll drive you back to your sorority house, Tobey."

"I'll walk her over," Larry offered. "It's right on my way and it's a nice night." He glanced at me questioningly.

"Okay," I agreed, as if it didn't make the slightest difference to me. But my heart was singing.

Funny how much prettier the campus looked by moonlight when you strolled along its paths with a boy instead of a couple of other girls. Larry and I didn't walk very fast and we talked a lot. It was amazing how congenial we were, how many of the same things we liked and how few we disagreed on. I felt a little sorry as the Theta House loomed ahead of us.

"This has been fun," Larry said.

"I enjoyed it, too," I admitted.

"Uh—" Larry hesitated a moment, eying me speculatively, "how about going out with me some night?"

"All right," I agreed, happiness swelling within me until I felt like a balloon about to burst.

"This dance my fraternity's having," Larry went on. "It will be three weeks from tonight. You free then?"

I nodded. When I could trust my voice, I said, "I'd love to go."

"Good!" Larry said. "It's a date. I'll give you a buzz before then, though. Maybe we can catch a movie or something. 'Night."

"Good night," I replied. "And thanks."

He lifted his hand and waved as he strode off down the walk. I turned and went up the steps and into the house, shutting the door quietly behind me. I was very calm and cool. But inside I was shouting with joy and turning cartwheels like crazy.

Well, I thought, well! Maybe I should go out baby-sitting more often if wonderful things like this could develop from it.

ten

Eve of the Dance

BEING A GIRL WHO HAD BEEN ASKED TO A FRATERNITY dance must have given me a special glow or something. Ted Chalmers, who sat behind me in English, walked all the way back to the house with me after Chapel on Sunday and asked me to go to the movies with him Friday night. And on Monday at dinner, Dave Johnsen managed to suggest, under cover of serving my dessert, that I go for a walk with him that evening and have a soda at the Barn.

"Without Baby?" I queried, smiling.

"Without Baby," Dave said firmly. "I'll walk her later. She needn't think she can tag along every time I go out with you."

Things were definitely picking up for me, just as Suz had been so sure they would. When I told her as much, she nodded, saying, "I wasn't worried about you for a minute." She frowned then, adding, "I know Larry Hartnett—that is, I know him by sight. He's in one of my classes."

"Don't you think he's attractive?" I asked.

Suz nodded. "Lots of other girls must think so, too.

He's always got one in tow. Quite a ladies' man, I should say."

"That makes it all the more flattering," I pointed out, "to have him invite me to his dance."

"I suppose so," Suz said. "But I like Dave better."

"I like him, too," I admitted, "but that doesn't stop me from liking Larry and Ted. And, of course, there's still Brose," I added, smiling, "even if his letters are horrible."

"Doesn't sound as if you're in any danger of concentrating too narrowly." Suz smiled, too. "But I feel sorry for poor Brose. After all, I can't write good letters, either."

"I'm not really holding it against him," I told her. "I've just sort of filed him away in my mind for future reference. When we get together at Christmas, he'll be fine. He shows up much better on a person-to-person basis."

A couple of days later I ran into my brother-in-law in the school bookstore, where I was buying some notebook paper.

"Say, you know what?" Adam accosted me. "The Hartnetts' baby has chicken pox. Alicia was going to call and tell you, but she said you must have had it when you were little, so it wouldn't make any difference to you."

"So that's why he seemed feverish," I said. "Yes, I'm sure I had it. The year I was in first grade I caught everything that went around. How is poor little Chris?"

"Oh, he's okay," Adam said, "except for being all broken out in red spots. It's Jinny who's having a heck of a time. It doesn't seem to have affected his pep a bit."

When Larry phoned and asked me to go bowling

Saturday night, I accepted with enthusiasm. During the course of our conversation, he, too, told me about Chris.

"I hope you've had chicken pox." My tone was a shade apprehensive, thinking ahead to his fraternity dance now only two weeks off.

"Oh, sure," Larry said. "Everybody's had chicken pox. I had to be different and get it in high school, so I've got some very clear memories of the way I looked. Poor Chris!"

There were six of us on the bowling date and it was a lot of fun. My days seemed to be speeding past much more quickly now. Between studies and pledge duties and occasional dates, I was really kept busy. Early in October we had our formal pledging party, a most impressive ceremony with all of us pledges dressed in white. And we got our pledge pins, which we would wear until February when we would be initiated into full membership in the Thetas and get our regular gold-and-pearl sorority pins.

"And then," Marilyn put it flatly, "we'll be free women and not have to run at everybody's beck and call."

"Just wait till next year," I reminded her, "then you can have new pledges waiting on you."

"I intend to take full advantage of them, too," my roommate said. And she'd be just the girl to do it, I thought.

Both of us were learning, along with the other pledges, that there was more to being a Theta than just living in the sorority house. Each of the sororities at Central had a particular charitable or civic enterprise to which the members devoted some of their time and energies. There was a nursery for the children of working mothers in the town at which some of the girls helped out. Others wrote letters for men in the nearby veteran's hospital, or put on skits to entertain them, or more ambitious shows to raise money for gifts for these disabled men. The Thetas' pet project centered around the Old People's Home on the outskirts of town. We knit laprobes and scarves for them. We made gay little tray favors for those who were too ill to eat in the regular dining room. Looking ahead toward Thanksgiving, we were making place cards in the shape of turkeys, and planning a big bridge party to raise money for some special treats for the holiday. But the big push, the older Thetas informed us, would be Christmas, when we always tried to do something really special for these old people who, in many cases, had no families to remember them.

Geri explained, "Some of us always try to go out and give them a little personal attention at Thanksgiving and Christmas. Not right on the very day, of course, since we're usually not here at that time. But we plan a party or something a few days ahead and they really seem to appreciate it."

Afterward, Marilyn confided to me, "I'll bet they wish all the unpleasant jobs on us pledges. They'll want us to be the ones who go out and visit the Home in person. And I hate being with people who are old and sick."

"Did it ever occur to you," I couldn't help asking, "that you might be old and sick yourself sometime? How can you be so selfish?"

Marilyn looked a bit startled. Usually, I just let her complaints slide over me, but this time I was pretty mad. It seemed to me that the Theta project was rather wonderful and I hated her being nasty about it.

"I'd think," I went on, "we should all be proud to have some part in a thing like this. Instead of being afraid you might have some job wished on you that you don't care for, why don't you forget about yourself for a change and think of someone less fortunate!"

I stopped, having gone a bit farther than I'd intended. But after all, she had it coming. Marilyn stood there, staring at me for a moment, while I waited for her to hit the ceiling. But then, instead of tearing into me, she said quite meekly, "Well, I suppose that is the right way to look at it. But I can't help it that I don't care for old people."

"Have you ever been around any?" I asked. "Some of them are awfully interesting."

I was thinking especially of Adam Wentworth's aunt, Miss Tess, who lived all alone in a great gingerbready house in Edgewood and whom I liked very much.

"Well, no," Marilyn admitted. "My grandparents are dead. And I've never been around old people, really, but I'm sure . . ."

"You're not sure at all," I interrupted. "It might do you good to visit the Old People's Home and find out that they can still be human even if they aren't young any more."

I guess I sounded so positive that Marilyn decided she'd be wasting her breath to argue with me. All she said was, "Well, there's no use getting so mad, Tobey. Of course, I'll do my share. But I don't have to be keen on it, do I?"

We left it at that. I thought Marilyn might harbor a grudge against me for the way I'd lit into her. But, curiously enough, we seemed to get on somewhat better after my outburst. Maybe, I thought, she might not be so selfish if someone took the trouble of setting her straight now and then, instead of just making the best of her difficult attitude.

Marilyn had been invited to the Sigma dance, too, but she was quite impressed when she heard that I was going with Larry Hartnett. It seemed that Suz had been correct in her estimate of Larry. There were a lot of girls who found him most attractive.

"How did he happen to ask you?" Marilyn queried in her blunt, tactless way. "Any of the junior or senior women would jump if he so much as crooked his finger at them."

"Maybe he was won by my youth," I said solemnly, "or the fact that I'm so devastatingly beautiful. He didn't say which."

"Okay." Marilyn smiled. But there was still a look of speculation in her eyes. "I didn't even know you knew him."

"Oh, yes," I said. "We met at the home of some married friends, Jinny and Gil Hartnett. Gil is Larry's older brother." I'd be darned if I'd admit I'd been babysitting at the time and have Marilyn feeling superior because that was the best thing I could find to do on a Saturday night.

"Well, all I can say is, you're real lucky," my roommate said, and sighed. "I wouldn't mind having a date with Larry Hartnett myself."

Over my dead body, I thought. But I didn't say so. . . .

The Sigma dance was to be informal. I decided days ahead to wear my black velveteen jumper with the scoop neck and the full, full skirt that whirled so prettily over my crinoline petticoat. On Friday morning, as I was crossing the campus, my mind filled with details of shoes and accessories, I ran into Dave Johnsen.

"Just the girl I want to see," he greeted me. "I came into a couple of bucks unexpected wealth for a little handy-man job I did for the Dean. How about helping me squander it at the movies tomorrow night?"

I felt a real pang of regret to have to turn him down. At the same time pride swelled in me at the realization that for the first time since I'd come to college, two men had asked me to go out on the same night.

"Gee, I'm sorry, Dave," I told him. "But I'm going to the Sigma dance."

"Oh," Dave's tone was philosophic. "Well, I'd hardly expect you to turn that down for a movie. Better luck next time." He lifted his hand in a farewell wave and went on his way.

That night I washed my hair and did my nails, which I had managed with great effort to keep long and glamorous. I was going to look my very best at the dance, or die in the attempt. Just before bed time, all the Thetas who weren't out on dates crowded into Peggy Martin's room in pajamas and pin curls. It was her birthday so we helped devour the luscious chocolate cake her mother had sent for the occasion. Someone was always having a birthday around the sorority house and we always had these chummy little celebrations. I enjoyed the party fairly well, but for some reason or other, I wasn't very hungry. Maybe I'd eaten too much dinner, I decided, or else it was the excitement of tomorrow night looming ahead. Several of the girls were going to the dance, so it was the main topic of conversation. And I was the target for many envious looks and some wistfully regretful remarks because I was going with Larry. Naturally I enjoyed both to the full.

Peggy's room got awfully warm and close with so many

people in it. When my head started to ache I said good night and went back to my own room and to bed. But despite my determination to get a good night's sleep, I kept waking fitfully and having the darndest dreams. I heard Marilyn come in and get into bed quietly so as not to waken me. And I pretended to be asleep, because I didn't want to get involved in conversation. If I didn't go to sleep, I thought desperately, I'd look an absolute hag for the dance. Finally, I dropped off again and dreamed a long, fantastic nightmare about being caught in a burning building. I had to make my escape down an endless ladder, wrapped in a scratchy wool blanket that made me itch all over. When I woke up, the dream still seemed so real to me that I actually felt hot and itchy. I peered out the window at the pale dawn light. It was still much too early to get up for keeps, but I simply had to have a drink of water. My throat felt parched.

I put my feet over the side of the bed and groped my way out of the room and down the hall to the bath for a drink. I didn't turn on any lights until I was inside the bathroom. No use waking anyone else at this ungodly hour. Touching the switch, I shut my eyes tight for a minute against the sudden stab of brilliance, then opened them in two squinting slits. A cry of dismay escaped me and I stood there, arrested by the appalling sight of my own image in the medicine-cabinet mirror. I knew it must be I, because it was I who had got out of bed and gone to the bathroom for a drink. But otherwise I would never have recognized the flushed, red-polka-dotted horror who stared back at me as Tobey Heydon.

eleven

Thanksgiving

IN TWO WEEKS I WAS AS GOOD AS NEW.

Looking back from the vantage point of my final days of convalescence, I could even smile at my jumbled recollections of being hastily bundled up and rushed over to the Infirmary by Mrs. Penn. Our housemother had clucked sympathetically over me, but she was understandably determined to get me out of the Theta House before anyone else contracted chicken pox. Only those girls whose rooms were closest to the bath had been aware of what was happening until I was safely ensconced in the contagious ward. When competent Doctor Matthews checked into the matter, it turned out that all the other Thetas had already had the silly disease. And for that I was grateful. If I'd started an epidemic around the sorority house, it would have been awful.

As it was, it was only awful for me.

"At least," Doctor Matthews, who was fairly young and very feminine and pretty, even in her starched white hospital jacket, teased me. "You're the only patient I've had who got a carnation corsage to dress up her pajamas."

It had been sweet of Larry to send me the flowers he'd

planned to give me for the dance. I appreciated them, even though it would have made me a smidgen happier if he'd stayed away from the dance himself instead of going stag. But I suppose that was too much to hope for. Besides the corsage, I got lots of other flowers. Yellow and white chrysanthemums from my sorority sisters. Roses from Alicia and Adam. Dave sent me chocolate peppermints, which he knew were my favorite candy, and a funny get-well card signed with Baby's large footprint. Suz brought over some whodunits when I began to feel better and I relaxed with these in between bouts with class work. And the Hartnetts felt so sorry about my having been infected by their child that Jinny kept me supplied with home-baked cookies, which she brought to the Infirmary every other day or so.

Along with the gifts, I was deluged with phone calls and mail, including a solicitous letter from my mother in which she corrected my mistaken idea that I'd already had chicken pox.

"It was practically the only thing you missed," Mom wrote, "so I suppose it was sure to catch up with you sooner or later."

I wished it might have been either sooner or later, but not right at this particular time. Still, I tried to remind myself cheerfully, there would be other dances, other dates. Larry phoned several times and so did Dave. And my sorority sisters were so faithful in relaying to me all that was going on around the house and on campus that I hardly felt left out of things at all.

By the time I was back in circulation again it was almost Thanksgiving. It had snowed while I was cooped up in the Infirmary and the chill of winter was in the air. All talk around college was of going home for the long

holiday week end. Home! The mere thought of it was
enough to make me feel happy and choked up and full
of anticipation. It didn't seem possible I'd been away
from my family for more than two months. My Saturdays had been so busy with pledge duties, and football
games, it had thrown a monkey wrench into my plan to
spend an occasional week end in Edgewood. With Brose
far away and no emergency making a trip home really
necessary, I'd been too absorbed in college life to pull
myself away. Still, the thought of Thanksgiving was
wonderful.

On the Saturday before the holiday, I had a date with
Larry Hartnett. He called it my coming out party and
we doubled with Marilyn and a fraternity brother of
Larry's named Russ Colvin. We drove the forty-odd
miles to Indianapolis, where we had dinner at a hotel
supper club and danced and saw a floor show. It was
definitely the most glamorous and expensive date I'd
had since I came to college. Larry and Russ didn't seem
to care how they spent money. No doubt it was the
contrast that started me thinking about Dave, who always had to count pennies so carefully. And then the
orchestra swung into a song that had been my and
Brose's favorite last summer and that started me thinking
about Brose. How fickle could you get, I wondered
guiltily? But I liked all three of them, there was no
denying that. And how was a girl supposed to learn
which man was really the one for her unless she took
advantage of her opportunity to know as many as possible? This thought quieted my conscience and I proceeded to have fun.

Later, lingering for a moment with Larry at the Theta
House door, it seemed the most natural thing in the

world to give him a good-night kiss. Marilyn was kissing Russ and this was their first date. So if I'd held
back when Larry leaned down toward me, it would have
seemed positively unfeeling, after the wonderful evening we'd had.

"This," Larry murmured, his voice low and husky and
for my ears alone, "could get to be habit forming!"

"Ummmm," I said ambiguously. This is a word, I
had discovered, which, if said in a dreamy enough tone,
lulls a man into thinking you are agreeing with him,
without your actually committing yourself. Larry didn't
stir me as Brose always did. Still, there was no denying
that my heart was beating a little faster.

When the boys had driven off and Marilyn and I had
gone upstairs and were getting ready for bed, I asked
her, "How did you like Russ?"

"He's all right," Marilyn conceded with a little shrug,
creaming her face conscientiously at the mirror. "Not
the type I'm mad for, but I liked the brand of entertainment offered."

"It was the first night club I've been to in ages," I
admitted, getting into my pajamas. Then I asked, prodded by curiosity, "What type do you really go for,
Marilyn?"

A faint smile curved my roommate's lips. "Larry,"
she said frankly. "He has enough attraction for two men.
What a shame he isn't twins."

"Then we could each have one of him—is that it?"

Marilyn turned from the mirror to face me. She was
beautiful even with her face all shiny and her hair
brushed back. "That would be cozy. But since he's
only one, you won't care if I try to get a date with him,
will you?"

At least, I thought, she was open enough about her intentions. I shook my head. "I haven't any strings on him. But you won't mind if I try to keep him happy enough so he won't ask you for a date, will you?" I could be frank and open, too.

Marilyn's eyes met mine in a long look of understanding. "Not at all," she said. "I just wanted you to know the score."

And with that she gave me a winning friendly smile. So I gave her a winning friendly smile and hurried into bed, so she'd be the one who had to turn off the light.

On Sunday I went to Chapel with Dave and he suggested we go ice skating that afternoon. There was a low section back of the Gym that the college had flooded early in November and it was frozen solid now and proved to be quite a popular spot. I hadn't been on skates yet this season, but after a few rather wobbling circles around the edge of the pond, clinging hard to Dave's hands for support, I began to hit my stride. It was fun after that. My self-confidence returned and Dave, who was a very good skater, led me through several intricate figures that made me feel like an Olympic champion. The sun shone brightly on all the colorful, graceful figures whipping along beside us. And the chill air turned my cheeks pink and seemed to fill me with a bouncy, exuberant sort of energy that made me willing to try anything. We skated till dusk, then stopped by at the Barn for hot chocolate to warm us.

"That was fun." I smiled at Dave across the narrow table. "You're really a terrific skater, almost professional."

Dave laughed. "A skating date, with hot chocolate

afterward," he informed me, "is one of the least expensive kinds a guy can have. So I've had a lot of practice. You're pretty good, too," he added. "How come?"

My smile widened. "The boy I like back home often didn't have much money, either. So we skated a good deal."

"What happened?" Dave queried. "Break up?"

I shook my head. "He went to Colorado to college. I won't see him till Christmas." I asked then, "Don't you have a girl back home, too?"

"Sort of." Dave grinned, his glance direct on mine. "Nothing serious. It'll be a long time before I can afford to get serious."

We talked of other things then, lots of other things, all interesting. But somehow the thought of Brose lingered in my mind. And I wondered if Dave, too, might be having a little trouble with his memories. Later, though, as we crossed the campus through the deep blue dusk, Dave held my hand tight in his and I could feel the warmth of his fingers even through our mittens. His touch drove Brose's ghost from my thoughts.

"It'll seem funny," Dave said, "not to see you from Wednesday till Monday. I've got kind of used to having you around."

I nodded, realizing that I'd miss him, too. But I said, "You'll be with your family and all your friends back home. You probably won't have time to give me a thought."

"Oh, I'll be busy," Dave agreed, "but I'll think of you."

We had reached the house then, and he pulled me close for a brief moment in an impulsive hug. Our skates clanked together like an alarm bell. Dave's cheek was cold and firm against mine as he held me. For a second I thought he was going to try for a kiss, but he didn't. Just gave my shoulder an affectionate pat as he let me go. My breath hurried a little just the same.

"I probably won't get a chance to see you alone again before the holiday," Dave said. "So be good and have fun."

"Oh, I will," I told him. "You, too, Dave. And thanks for this afternoon. I enjoyed it a lot."

"Yeah, me, too," Dave said. "See you, Tobey."

He strode off down the snowy sidewalk, his feet making crunching sounds. I hated, somehow, to see him go. . . .

Thanksgiving was wonderful, the homey, warmly hospitable sort of day it was meant to be. Eight of us sat down to a turkey dinner, complete with all the trimmings. There were Alicia and Adam and his father and great-aunt, Miss Tess Wentworth, besides Mom and Dad and Midge and me. All of us were very fond of Aunt Tess, who was quite old and fragile and rather eccentric, but sweet. I couldn't help remembering how a crowd of us Thetas had gone out to the Old People's Home near Central for a pre-holiday visit. We had taken along the favors we had made for their Thanksgiving dinner and some flowers and candy. Marilyn, who had complained so over having to go, had found to her surprise that she didn't have a bad time, after all. There was one quite courtly old gentleman who had been most taken with her. He had picked up her gloves when she dropped them and had told her with engaging frankness how pretty she was, a compliment which was bound to endear him to Marilyn. They had spent some time in lively conversation. We had stayed for a couple of hours, talking, singing old-time songs around their slightly out-of-tune piano, and visiting with them.

That experience made me understand exactly what Miss Tess meant when she told us, as we all sat in our living room after dinner, "Sometimes we old people have a feeling that we're just sitting on the side lines of life. Everything rushes past so quickly, it's hard for us to keep up. But when younger people take the trouble to include us in their activities, as you've done today, it gives us a sense of being a part of the present, as well as the past."

My sister Midge, who is especially fond of Miss Tess, leaned over to lay her hand affectionately on the thin blue-veined fingers of the old lady. Midge said with a little smile, "Now you're just hinting for a compliment. You know we like to have you here—it's more fun."

We all echoed the same thought in our different ways and Miss Tess looked so pleased it made my eyelids sting a little. I wished that every one of the old people at the Home had someone who could have included them in their holiday festivities. And I felt prouder than ever of my sorority for doing all it could.

When the mail came Friday morning, I was still in bed. It was such a luxury to sleep late. Midge brought me a letter from Brose, then perched cozily on the foot of my bed while I read it through. This didn't take long. But at least, it had been thoughtful of him to write me at home.

"Kind of short, wasn't it?" Midge asked.

I grinned at her. Midge had changed quite a bit in the past two months. I supposed it was the junior high influence. Instead of braids, she had her hair tied back in a pony tail. And instead of the inevitable blue jeans and tee-shirt she was wearing trim black denim toreador pants and a plaid gingham blouse with a lot of red and gray in it. Very becoming.

"Brose," I informed my little sister, "always writes short letters. The longest one I've had so far was one page. This is ten lines—that's a pretty good average."

"You're kidding," Midge said. "Has he got another girl, or something?"

"He might have," I admitted, "although he's never said anything about her. But I have some new boys, too, and I've never gone into detail about them in my letters to Brose. I don't believe that's why he writes short letters, though. It's just that he hates writing."

"Oh," Midge said. "I like to write letters myself."

"So do I," I told her, "but that doesn't mean everyone has to. And I certainly don't care any less for Brose just because he isn't very articulate on paper."

I smiled and my little sister smiled back at me. Suddenly I made a startling discovery.

"Your braces!" I exclaimed. "You aren't wearing them."

Midge shook her head delightedly in the negative. "Only a retainer while I sleep. I was wondering when you'd notice."

"So that's what makes you look so much prettier," I said.

It was quite true, she did look prettier. No braces on her teeth. A pony tail. Toreador pants. Everything added up to an undeniable total. My little sister was growing up.

twelve

Sisterly Advice

BARBIE—OR, RATHER, LYNN AND I GOT TOGETHER THAT afternoon for a good old gab session. She came over to our house and we settled down in the library in front of the fireplace, with a Black Cow apiece and a big plate of Mom's chocolate macaroons. Midge had gone off to a matinee with her pal, Judy Allen, and Mom was at her Friday afternoon bridge club. So Barbie and I had the place to ourselves and could really let our hair down.

"I'll never get used to calling you Lynn," I told her.

"It doesn't matter," Barbie said. "My family all call me Barbie, so I'm used to it. But I do think Lynn suits me better now, don't you?"

I nodded. Barbie looked a bit older, I thought, with her hair grown out fairly long from last summer's short cut, and brushed back from her face, so that her cheekbones seemed more prominent. Her black sweater, with the unusual silver pendant dangling against it, gave her a high-fashion look.

"You look older," Barbie said, "smoother. I like your hair that way, without bangs."

I burst out laughing. "Exactly what I was thinking about you," I told her and Barbie laughed, too.

"So we're a couple of ancient hags," she said, "after two months of college. What'll we look like after four years?"

Barbie hadn't changed really. Neither had I. Underneath our new hairdos and more sophisticated clothes, we were the same old friends. It was easy to pick up right where we had left off. She told me all about her school and the new men she'd met and all the exciting things that had happened. And I confided all my news to her. The funny thing was, as I told Barbie about Larry and Dave and some of my more exciting experiences, it sounded as though I'd been having a terrific whirl. Maybe I had, I realized, only it just hadn't seemed like it while it was going on. I told her about Suz and Marilyn and life around the Theta House. And she told me about her sorority and the friends she had made.

"How's Brose?" she asked finally.

So I explained how disappointing his letters had proved. "But at least," I finished, "we still write."

Barbie said, "It'll seem funny seeing him Christmas, I'll bet. You'll be like a couple of strangers."

I couldn't imagine feeling strange with Brose. On the other hand, I found it hard now to remember exactly how he looked. When I tried, I kept seeing a mental image of his graduation picture, which I had on my dresser at school, or the snapshot of him in his swimming trunks I'd taken on the beach at Green Lake last summer. Dave was much clearer in my mind, with his stubbly haircut and engaging grin. So was Larry, whose dark good looks were etched crystal-clear in my memory. But that, I told myself, was just because I'd seen both of them so much more recently. Or was it, a small voice deep within me asked?

Barbie said, "I was thinking of trying to get the old crowd together for a little party tomorrow night. But there are hardly any of us around."

"I know." I'd had the same idea until I started checking. Lots of the kids, like Brose, were at schools too far away to get back for a short holiday. And some colleges even had classes the Friday after Thanksgiving. "Maybe we can go to a movie together," I suggested, "and have a soda at Joe's afterward, for old times' sake."

"Okay," Barbie agreed.

Neither of us said it aloud, but I suspected she felt the same way I did. In spite of being happy to see my family, I'd be kind of glad to get back to school. That seemed the core of my life now. I had a queer sensation of marking time till I got back.

Midge came in from her matinee just after Barbie left. She followed me upstairs to my room and sat on my bed, her arms curled around her knees, watching me as I freshened my lipstick at the dressing-table mirror. I was struck by a sudden memory that made me smile. I used to curl up on Alicia's bed, or that of my older sister, Janet, in just that way, watching wistfully as they put on lipstick, anxious for the time to pass quickly so that I could be grown up, too, and live in the glamorous, only half-sensed world that they inhabited.

"How was the show?" I asked, my voice gentle.

Midge held her nose expressively. "A stinky Western," she said. "The boys liked it."

"Did you and Judy go with boys?" my brows lifted a little in surprise. After all, Midge is just in seventh grade.

" 'Course not," Midge shook her head. "We went

with three other girls. But some boys sat in the row right behind us." There was a note of pride in her voice, so I judged that this was important. She went on, "That way it's almost like dating. They know we're going to be there and we know they will, too."

"Oh," I nodded. I was remembering back to my own junior high days—how long ago they seemed! I asked, smiling, "What do they do, throw popcorn at you and pull your hair?"

Midge's eyes widened. "How'd you know?"

I had to laugh then, but Midge laughed, too, when she saw I was laughing with her, rather than at her. "Oh, I used to go to matinees, too."

"They say things to us, sometimes," Midge admitted confidentially, "funny things. Like today, when the guy was kissing the girl at the end of the picture, Kirby leaned over and said, 'This is a tender moment,' and we nearly died laughing." Midge admitted then a shade wistfully, " 'Course, he was really talking to Betty Lou, but I was sitting right next to her."

"Who is Kirby?" I asked. The name was unfamiliar.

"Kirby Carmichael," my sister said. Her voice positively caressed the syllables of his name. "He likes Betty Lou, though."

"Oh, well," I murmured, "boys are sort of fickle at that age. He may like you next."

"I don't think so," Midge shook her head. "Betty Lou's got real dark hair and it's naturally curly. Tobey," she asked, "while you're home will you show me how you pin your hair up in those little snails at night, so it gets real curly."

"Sure," I promised. A thought struck me then and I

asked, "What happened to Bobby who used to play with you so much?"

"You mean ol' Bob Pierson?" my sister inquired with vast disdain. "He's still around."

"Who does Bob like?"

"He hates girls," Midge informed me. "He thinks they're silly. At Fortnightly Club the teacher has to make him ask somebody to dance. Then he always picks me, just because we used to play together."

Ah, good old Fortnightly, I thought. How well I remembered that junior high dancing class and prim Miss Hildegarde who had charge of it. But I was more interested in Bob at the moment. I asked Midge, "Does he still stop by for you on his way to school?"

"Sometimes." Midge shrugged casually. "He has to go right past the house. But he never carries my books or anything, like Kirby does Betty Lou's."

"He doesn't?" I was glad dusk was deepening beyond the windows, so that my room was fairly dark. I wouldn't want Midge to realize my inner amusement. "Some boys are like that," I went on gravely. "They take longer to grow up than girls do."

"I don't think he'll ever grow up," my sister said. "Not that I care, personally. But you know what he did last summer?"

I shook my head.

"He put a caterpillar down my neck," Midge stated in outraged accents. "The big old baby!"

I swallowed a laugh and pointed out, "Couldn't that just have been his way of attracting your attention?"

"Ol' Bob Pierson?" Midge stared at me in astonishment. "You mean he might have done it because he's interested in me as a girl?" Then, at my nod, she emitted a derisive snort of laughter. "Not him," she stated positively. "I don't think he even knows I am a girl, or, if he does, he doesn't care. Our friendship," she informed me, "is strictly platoonic."

"Platonic, honey," I corrected gently. "Anyway, that's the way friendships should be at your age, don't you think?"

"I guess so," my sister's frown was doubtful. "That's what Mom says, too. But some of the kids are going steady."

"In junior high?" I gasped.

"Sure," Midge nodded. "Kirby and Betty Lou practically are. He gets awful mad if she pays attention to any other boy."

"For pity's sake!" I said weakly. "Things must be moving fast these days. Brose and I were halfway through high school before we got any such notions. And then it didn't last very long."

"You mean you didn't like going steady?" Midge sounded surprised.

I shook my head with a little smile. "Playing the field's a lot more fun. Oh, Brose was always my favorite, but I dated other fellows, too. Don't you remember?"

She nodded slowly. "Yeah—but—"

"But, what?" I prodded as she stopped.

"Well, it's just that when you're going steady you must have such a—well, such a secure kind of feeling. I mean—well, take at Fortnightly. There's more girls than boys and some of us girls always have to dance together. But Kirby always asks Betty Lou and it's that way with all the kids that go steady, unless Miss Hildegarde makes it a Scramble Dance."

We seemed to keep getting back to Fortnightly. It

wasn't so far behind me that I'd forgotten the hot, panicky feeling you could get, sitting there on one of the chairs at the side of the junior high gym, watching the boys make a beeline for the six or so most popular girls, hoping that you'd be chosen by someone who wasn't too impossible. Midge looked up at me and I think she must have sensed my sympathy and understanding.

"Sometimes," I told her ruefully, "it isn't the easiest thing in the world to be a girl. Boys always get to do the picking. That's just something we have to get used to. But I don't think going steady's the solution."

"It doesn't usually last very long." Midge's tone was wistful, almost coaxing, as though she wanted my approval. "You go steady with one boy for a few weeks and then with someone else."

"I know," I said. I remembered, although I'd been in high school when I'd had to decide about it. "But I still think it's pretty stupid."

After a minute's thought my sister admitted, "I guess I do, too, really. I mean, I can't think of anybody I'd want to go steady with."

"Of course you can't." I got up from the dressing table and went over to sit beside her. "Why, even at my age, I'm not sure which boy I like best. I think it's Brose, but we decided it was best to go to different colleges, so we'd have a chance to be sure. And we're both dating other people—if our feeling for each other can't stand that, it isn't worth much."

Never could I remember having talked so seriously with Midge before. She looked at me solemnly, her blue eyes wide and interested. It occurred to me that Midge was being gypped a little, being the youngest in the family. With me away at college, she might as well have been an only child. When I was her age, I'd had Alicia and Janet to watch and copy and pick up ideas from. Being one of the middle ones in a family of four girls was quite a liberal education in itself.

Midge said, "Gee, Tobey, I wish you were around to talk to all the time. It never used to seem this way before."

"Of course, it didn't," I told her, laughing a little. "That's because you were just a little kid, but you're getting older now. That makes us have more in common."

"Yeah," she agreed, smiling, too, her eyes brightening.

"Let's not have any more of this worrying for fear you aren't going to be popular," I told her. "You're getting prettier all the time and if you quit thinking so much about yourself and act natural and friendly with the boys, they're bound to like you."

"Honest?"

"Honest!" I said firmly.

Midge sat thoughtfully for a moment. Then she said, "Tobey?"

"Yes?"

"When you go back to college, can I write you for advice when anything comes up—about boys or any-thing—that I'm not sure about?"

"You do that," I told her. "And I'll answer right away."

"I can ask Mom, of course," Midge admitted. "She knows, too. But you've lived through it all so much more recently."

"I'm still living through it," I admitted.

"Growing up, you mean?" Midge asked.

I nodded. "You're on the lower edge of it and I'm on the upper. And you know what?"

"What?"

"It's fun," I whispered and we both burst out laughing.

thirteen

Disappointment

BACK AT COLLEGE, IT WAS EASY TO GET INTO THE SWING of things once more. In fact, after a couple of days, it seemed as if I'd never been away. Studies occupied much of my time. All the instructors seemed bent on giving as heavy assignments as possible, paving the way for Christmas vacation, which was less than a month away now. And the Thetas were determined that we pledges keep our grade average high enough so that we'd be a credit to our sorority.

Even without their prodding, I'd have wanted to do my best. I was finding my subjects stimulating and I liked most of my professors, some better than others naturally. College seemed to be arousing my intellectual curiosity in directions I'd never bothered to explore in high school.

Besides our studies, we were busy around the Theta house with preparations for the Christmas party we would be giving at the Old People's Home. We were making little gifts for each of them and practicing up on our carol singing for their entertainment. But even while we studied and worked on our sorority project, there was another matter that we discussed endlessly and which occupied a good share of our thoughts.

That was the Inter-Fraternity Dance.

By far the biggest social event of the fall term, it was being held later than usual this year, on the Friday preceding the start of the Christmas holiday. Last year, as I well remembered, it had taken place on the Thanksgiving week end and there had been a football game in connection with it. The Central team had played its Thanksgiving game at another college this year, so a later date had been chosen for the Inter-Fraternity.

Last year I had been Dick Allen's guest for the occasion. I didn't suppose I'd ever forget what fun we'd had. Now Dick was in the navy and the last I'd heard from him had been a card with a Panama postmark months ago. And who would ask me to the big dance this year? That was a question that loomed large in my mind. Or would I get to go at all? That question loomed even larger.

Logical reflection had convinced me that Larry Hartnett was my best possibility. Dave wouldn't have that much money to spend. There were a couple of outside chances, men I'd dated once or twice. But my hopes were really hung on Larry.

Lots of the Thetas already had dates set for the Inter-Fraternity. Each time I heard of another one, a small chill wind blew across my heart. The magic night was only three weeks off now. With every passing day, I grew more anxious.

Suz was sympathetic when I confided my misgivings to her over a cup of hot chocolate at the Barn. She told me, "I'll keep my fingers crossed for you. I suppose, though, that a girl can never feel too sure with a guy of

Larry's type. He's too popular to count on. Now if it were Dave—"

I didn't even let her finish that avenue of useless speculation. "Can you imagine Dave having enough money to take in a big, expensive wing-ding like the Inter-Fraternity?"

"Well—no," Suz had to admit.

"Whenever I run into Larry," I brooded aloud, "he's real friendly. We've had one date since Thanksgiving, but he didn't say a word about the dance."

Suz's glance was pitying. "In a way," she said, "I guess I'm lucky. I know I haven't a chance of getting invited, so I don't get my hopes up. I'm resigned to my fate. But it's different for you, harder."

Suddenly I felt ashamed of myself. Here I was, complaining to Suz, when I was having ever so much more fun at college than she. If I didn't watch out, I'd be as bad as Marilyn, never seeing anyone else's problems but my own.

I looked at Suz a trifle shamefacedly. "You've got about as much hope of getting there as I have," I told her. "But there's no reason I should weep on your shoulder about it. If I mention the Inter-Fraternity again, bop me one, will you?"

"No." Suz smiled at me. "But I do feel you're starting to take a more reasonable attitude about it."

Down inside, though, I was still hoping hard.

When I got back to the Theta House, there was a letter from Brose on the hall table. I glanced hopefully at the note pad beside the telephone, but there was no record of any call for me. Up in my room, I flopped down on the bed to read my letter. It was, I discovered as soon as I opened it, the longest one he had written yet. His big familiar scrawl quite filled the first page and spilled over almost to the bottom of the second.

Well! I thought. Well! This is more like it.

I couldn't help wondering what had happened to give him so much to write about. It didn't take me long to find out. He skimmed over his parents' visit to him on Thanksgiving in a few lines and then launched into a quite detailed description of the big dance his fraternity had given the first Saturday in December. He had served on the dance committee and he gave me a full run-down on the decorations, the orchestra and so on, along with quite a bit of description about the dance itself and what a success it had been. As a sort of afterthought, or merely because he knew darned well I'd be curious, he added the further information that he had taken a girl named Jan Shelby to the dance and that she had been one of the beauty queen's court of attendants. "But," he had finished, "she isn't nearly as cute as you, Tobey. And I don't like her half as well, although she's a nice kid. Gee, I can hardly wait till Christmas, when I'll be seeing you."

I read the letter through twice, then put it away thoughtfully in my dresser drawer. Jan Shelby—what a pretty name. And she must be a very pretty girl, too, or she wouldn't have been in the queen's court. I wondered if this had been Brose's first date with her. Probably not, although he hadn't mentioned her before. In one way I was glad and in another sorry. Now, instead of just a vague, impersonal idea of the girls he was meeting out in Colorado, I had a name and a face. Oh, yes, I immediately conjured up a full set of features, hair, eyes, everything to fill in the bare outline Brose had given me. Jan Shelby was fair, I felt sure, because Brose

had always been a pushover for blondes. Look at the
way he'd fallen for Kentucky Jackson ages ago, and the
weakness he'd developed for Clarissa Hyde when she
and her mother visited his family last summer. Now
that I considered the matter, I decided that Jan probably resembled one or the other of them and my heart
fell so far it made a sort of dull thud deep down inside
of me. The thought of Brose being exposed to someone so attractive was awful. Suddenly I wished he'd
stuck to his short, uncommunicative letters. At least,
when he wrote only a few lines, he didn't give me so
much to think about and worry over.

Of course, I realized, I wouldn't have felt nearly so
bad over his disclosures if I'd been more confident of
being invited to the Inter-Fraternity. But uncertainty
gnawed at me. And that, coupled with the thought of
Brose having a wonderful time with another girl at his
big dance, was almost too much to bear.

I tried to forget about his letter and about Larry Hartnett and everything else that was bothering me and con-
centrate on my next day's assignment in English Comp.
But even surrounded by class notes and reference books,
I couldn't seem to lose myself completely in my work.
I chewed my pen and wondered wistfully whether Larry
might be getting ready to phone me this minute. I
could almost hear the tone of his voice as he asked,
"About the Inter-Fraternity, Tobey, will you go with
me?" Would I? My spirits soared at the very thought.
But they fell again when I got to wondering whether
Jan Shelby had that same fiendish trick of looking up at
a boy from beneath her fantastic eyelashes and drawling,
"That's suh-weet of you," that Clarissa had practiced so
devastatingly.

I was finally winning my bout with English com-
position when the door opened and Marilyn came in.
"Hi," I greeted her with a smile.

My roommate and I had been getting along very
well lately. It was my secret opinion that the Thetas
were having a good influence on her, even if it hadn't
been the sorority she wanted. She was doing her share
of work on our projects with better grace these days
and complaining considerably less than she used to.
But now, instead of responding to my smile, her brows
drew together in a frown and she looked positively
stormy.

"I'm so mad I could pop!" she exclaimed, shrugging
off her bright red jacket. "You will be, too, when I tell
you."

She proceeded to do so, her words crackling with in-
dignation. It seemed she and Russ Colvin had just
stopped at the Barn for a soda and, since he was taking
her to the Inter-Fraternity, they had naturally got to
talking about that. "And you know what he told me,
quite casually and as though it weren't of the slightest
importance?" Marilyn demanded, something almost like
sympathy softening the angry sparkle of her eyes.

I shook my head, apprehension settling over me.

"Larry has invited a girl from his home town here for
the dance—someone he used to date in high school."

Well, there it was, definite and inescapable. No use
hoping any more. I wasn't going to get to go to the
Inter-Fraternity. Might as well face the stark fact and
try to adjust to it. Marilyn was still talking, saying
what she thought of Larry for pulling such a low trick.
Of course, I realized wryly, if he had asked her to go,
she'd have jumped at the chance. And she wouldn't have

felt he was treating me so unfairly then. It was the thought of his passing us both up, along with all the other girls around college who were mad about him, that made her so angry.

I didn't feel angry at all—just hurt and sick with disappointment. After all, Larry had a right to date any girl he chose. He couldn't help it if I had made him the peg on which to hang all my hopes. I really had no one but myself to blame, knowing perfectly well how popular he was and how he liked to play the field.

When Marilyn began to run down, so that I could get a word in, I said as much.

"How can you be philosophical about it?" she demanded.

"I'm not really," I admitted. "I'm disappointed as the dickens. But I still don't think I have anything to blame Larry for." I couldn't help smiling a little as a sudden memory struck me. "Maybe Fate's paying me back for doing this same trick to some other girl last year." I told her then about being asked to the Inter-Fraternity while I was still in high school, mainly because Dick Allen had had a scrap with his regular girl at college and asked me instead.

"But you and Larry haven't had a scrap," Marilyn argued.

"I know," I agreed. "But I haven't any strings on him."

There were a lot of other girls around college who weren't going to the big dance. It wasn't as if I didn't have company. But somehow that didn't seem to make it any easier, although I tried to convince myself it should.

The trouble was, so many of the Thetas were going,

it was the main topic of conversation around the house.
And even some of those who hadn't been asked yet remained hopeful. After all, it was still two weeks off, they
reminded themselves and each other with an optimism
which I secretly found pathetic.

When I answered Brose's letter, I told him about the
advance plans for the Inter-Fraternity. It would be
called Star Magic and the decorations sounded fabulous
and there would be a big name band. I didn't write
that I was going, but I didn't say I wasn't, either. Let
him think I was holding out on him if he liked. It
wouldn't be so hard on my pride as a straight admission
that I hadn't been invited and wasn't going to be.

Darn Larry anyway, I thought, whether it was reasonable or not!

One Friday night at dinner, Dave leaned down as he
served my dessert and inquired, "Busy tonight?"

I shook my head. I hadn't seen much of Dave since
the Thanksgiving holiday. This was understandable, of
course, since he was always so broke and busy. A couple
of times we'd walked Baby together. And I always enjoyed his company, even with a St. Bernard pulling us
enthusiastically along.

"How about a Coke at the Barn around eight?"

"Love to," I agreed, smiling.

A warm little feeling of pleasure settled over me at
the thought of the evening ahead. There was no denying that Dave was fun and that I liked him. Maybe he
could take my mind off my brooding regret over missing
the Inter-Fraternity.

fourteen

Surprise

DAVE WAS WEARING HIS STORM JACKET AND SNOW HAD dampened the crisp stubble of his hair when he called for me later that evening. When he had helped me with my coat, we went out together into the chill darkness. The sky was gray velvet and the night so still you could hear sounds from clear across the campus. The light but persistent snow left star patterns on our coats and felt wet and refreshing against our faces. Drifted snow lay blue-white all about us, accented by the yellow squares of lighted windows.

We walked along, our clasped hands swinging between us, our boots making crunching noises in the stillness. "How's Baby?" I asked.

"In disgrace at the moment," Dave chuckled. "She chewed up our housemother's hat. None of us thought it was very becoming, but Baby's the only one who offered any really constructive criticism. Now Mrs. Tilden will have to get a new one and maybe we'll like it better."

"Poor Baby," I laughed. "What did Mrs. Tilden do to her?"

"Oh, she talked real severe," Dave admitted, "and

threatened to keep Baby in the kitchen. But, of course, she won't. The dog's so big she can reach the tops of the tables and cabinets. She's more of a menace in the kitchen than anywhere else. And Mrs. Tilden's actually just as silly about her as the rest of us are."

The stretches of unbroken snow on all sides summoned up happy memories. "Wouldn't that be wonderful for a game of Fox and Geese?" I queried pointing.

"Sure." Dave grinned. "Let's play."

So we both jogged around in a big circle, then in to the center for the spokes of the wheel. "Now you're it!" I told Dave, darting away from him.

He chased me till we were both breathless. But I kept getting into "home" in the center of the circle each time I was in danger of getting caught. "Let's call it a draw," I gasped finally. And Dave agreed, breathing as hard as I was.

"Did you ever make angels?" he asked.

"Oh, yes!" I exclaimed. "I loved to! Let's!"

So we each picked an untrampled spot and lay down on our backs, moving our arms up and down carefully to make the effect of wings. When Dave had pulled me to my feet again and brushed the snow off my back, I helped him get rid of the feathery whiteness that had lodged on his clothes. Then we began arguing over whose angel was best.

"Mine has more personality," I insisted, laughing.

But Dave felt his was more artistic.

As we left them to walk on toward the Barn, I told him, "If someone comes along and sees those and our Fox and Geese circle, they'll think we're nuts."

"Let them," Dave said. "What this poor old world needs is more crazy people like us. If we feel a sudden yen to play kid games, we do it. We're not in a rut. Why, some people are so conventional, they're incapable of relaxing and just having silly fun for fear it isn't the thing to do. I feel sorry for them."

"So do I." I replied. "They think they have to do whatever their crowd does, whether they really enjoy it or not, for fear people will think they're naive or something."

"I know," Dave agreed and we were both serious now. "A lot of the under-cover drinking and stuff that goes on—it's just the herd instinct, if you ask me. What are they trying to prove? There are sensible ways of convincing people you're mature. And you know another thing that bothers me about our generation?"

I shook my head.

"Their yen for security," Dave said. "You should hear some of the talk in the bull sessions. Fellows in their twenties and younger discussing what line of work will offer them the greatest security. Whether they should make a career of the army, because then they can get retired pay at such and such an age. Whether they should go with some big corporation when they graduate because of the retirement benefits. It makes me," Dave finished succinctly, "sick at my stomach."

"You talk like my father," I told him. "He says youth is the time for adventure, for new experiences, for taking reasonable risks. He gets so furious at all this planning for taking care of people from the cradle to the grave. And so do I," I added. "I don't know what we're afraid of, unless it's that we haven't got the fortitude to make our own security."

"That's just it," Dave said. "In the final analysis

security isn't anything anyone can give you, except your-self. It's—your own inner conviction that you can cope with whatever life brings. If you're sure of that, what have you got to worry about?"

"Not a thing," I agreed.

We had reached the Barn by that time and we went from the cold clear darkness into warmth and light and laughter. The juke box was playing and across the room a big bright-colored poster advertised the Inter-Fraternity Dance. I hadn't thought of it all the time I'd been in Dave's company, I realized. Why did the poster have to remind me?

We spoke to several people we knew and Dave found an empty booth and brought over a Coke for each of us. "I'm glad we settled all the world's problems before we got here." He chuckled as he slid in opposite me. "This atmosphere doesn't encourage heavy thinking."

"It's fun, though." I felt at home in the Barn now.

Dave nodded. He seemed, I thought, slightly diffident and quiet as we sipped our drinks. I'd never known him to be at a loss for words, not that the silence between us really bothered me. We were too good friends for that.

Suddenly Dave said, "I suppose you've got a date for the Inter-Fraternity?"

It wasn't like him to be unkind. But, I realized, he couldn't know he was rubbing salt into an unhealed wound. I swallowed. And then I managed, "Well— no—" I couldn't even think of anything witty and casual to add to my admission.

"You haven't?"

He didn't need to sound so pleased about it, I thought, even if it did mean I'd have the evening free to go for a walk with him, or perhaps see a movie, which was the most expensive sort of entertainment Dave could ever offer.

"Gee," he said happily, "that's more than I dared to hope for. How about going to the dance with me, Tobey?"

My heart leaped so it seemed to catch in my throat and make my voice sound choked. "With—you?" I gulped. "But—how—"

Dave burst out laughing and it was such a contagious thing I had to join in. "How did I get the price?" he finished my sentence. "I don't wonder you're surprised. Old Empty-pockets Johnsen coming through with a bid to the Inter-Fraternity. It staggers the imagination, doesn't it?"

"Well, yes," I had to admit. "But before you go any farther let me accept your invitation. I'd love to go with you."

"Good!" Dave grinned, his blue eyes bright and happy. "Now wouldn't you like to hear how it happened?" At my nod, he launched into an explanation that convinced me Cinderella wasn't the only one who had a fairy godmother.

"You remember my grandfather I told you about, the one who paints for his own enjoyment? Well, he's a carpenter, too, you know, and he was helping build a new wing onto a big house in our town. There was an interior decorator buzzing around the place, and she and Grandpop got to talking. She was trying to figure out the type of painting she could find to fit the room and go with the color scheme she had in mind. So Grandpop told her he had one. Well, the upshot was, she went over and looked at his paintings and went absolutely crazy about them. Grandpop thinks she went crazy, period." Dave chuckled. "But he's happy about the whole thing. This decorator wants to act as his agent. She's already sold a couple of his pictures and says she can sell all he'll do. She claims he's a primitive like Grandma Moses, only with a flair for color like Van Gogh thrown in for good measure. So," Dave finished, beaming, "Grandpop felt a wild urge to share his good fortune with the rest of the family. He sent me a check for twenty-five bucks, with the sole stipulation that I was to spend it on pure unadulterated pleasure and riotous living. So I couldn't think of a better use for it than to take you to the Inter-Fraternity—only I was scared maybe it had come too late."

"I'm glad it didn't," I assured him warmly.

There wasn't anyone I'd rather go to the dance with than Dave. The way things had worked out, I was glad Larry hadn't asked me. Let his hometown girl have him, I thought happily. She was quite welcome. . . .

The Theta Christmas party out at the Old People's Home was a big success. Our gifts were most welcome and I couldn't help wondering, with a slightly choky feeling, whether some of the elderly people would be getting any other gifts at all. It must be so sad, I thought, to be old and alone, without any family to make a fuss over you and give you a feeling of importance, of being needed. The Home was quite a comfortable, pleasant sort of place and the people in charge were kindly. Still, it wasn't like being in your own home, with family or close friends about.

But, for this night at least, everyone felt important. I was proud of my sorority as I saw all the girls putting themselves out to be agreeable and thoughtful, to see that all the old people were included in each activity, that they had fun. Marilyn, I noted, was doing her share, or more. Was this the girl, I thought amusedly, who had felt she didn't like old people? Marilyn was changing, improving. There was no doubt of it in my mind any more. And I was glad.

There was a tree, gay with tinsel and colored lights and ornaments. There were sweet familiar carols around the piano. And there were the Christmas cookies we had baked in the sorority kitchen under Nippy's cheerful supervision and which were now being served with coffee and hot chocolate. Tomorrow, I realized, all of us Thetas would be intent on our own affairs once more. But I didn't see how any of us could forget tonight.

I was surprised and pleased to hear Marilyn suggest, as we were driving back to college, "Can't we do a little more for them during the rest of the year? How about their birthdays? I'll bet a lot of them never even get a card. And it would be easy for us to find out the dates from the matron."

Everyone agreed that was a wonderful idea. Suggestions flew back and forth as the bus sped through the winter night. Before we were back at the Theta House, Marilyn and Geri Clair and I had been picked to work out the details of this further project. Not for the first time, I felt thankful deep down inside that I was pledged to the Thetas.

This was such a busy time of year, the days raced past too quickly. And yet, in another way, they seemed to drag when I started looking ahead to the holidays and thinking about getting to see Brose again. Would he still like me, I wondered? Would I still like him?

How had the other people both of us had dated affected our relationship? I would just have to wait till we met again before I could tell what three months apart had done to us.

On the night of the Inter-Fraternity, the Theta House was in a state of mad upheaval from dinner time on. Those who weren't going to the dance had made plans of their own so they wouldn't be around. The rest of us clogged the shower rooms and chased through the halls half dressed, borrowing jewelry and nail polish and crinolines, shrieking excitedly. It was just like last year, I remembered, only now I was a part of it as I hadn't been when I had been a guest for the week end.

When Dave was announced, I went down the stairs secure in the knowledge that my dark green formal did a lot for me. Dave's blue eyes widened appreciatively and his lips formed a soundless, but eloquent, whistle of approval. He had brought me a lovely corsage of yellow rosebuds. As I thanked him and pinned the flowers to the collar of my coat, I realized that Dave, too, looked quite special tonight. His rented dinner jacket fitted his broad shoulders nicely and his clear complexion glowed fresh from the cold. There was an air of anticipation about him and it struck me that a big dance like this one was an unusual experience for him. I knew he hadn't had the money to go to any others during all his months at college. A firm determination to make tonight as wonderful an occasion as possible for him grew in me. We were both going to have fun!

I'm not sure whether it was due to Dave, or my own attitude, but the Inter-Fraternity proved to be one of the nicest dances I'd ever attended. And I'd gone to a good many. The decorations were lovely, great silver stars and moons and a large mirrored ball that hung from the middle of the ceiling and revolved to cast flickers of light and shadow across the dancers. The music was terrific and Dave quite a good dancer. Not as smooth as Brose, I thought, but rather better than Larry.

"You're a wonderful dancer," I told him.

"You're only saying that because it's true," Dave said, then grinned. But he added, his tone low and personal, "Anyone could dance with you, Tobey."

It was a happy unforgettable night for both of us. Walking back to the Theta House through a white fairyland of snow, Dave held my hand and told me he was going to miss me over Christmas.

"I'll miss you, too," I said. And I meant it. Still, his mention of Christmas started all the questions about Brose flying around in my mind like butterflies. Would we or wouldn't we feel the same toward each other? Even Dave's light, undemanding good-night kiss couldn't quite dispel that nagging question from my thoughts.

fifteen

Home for Christmas

CHRISTMAS HOLIDAYS STARTED ON WEDNESDAY, ALMOST A week before the big day itself. I drove home with Alicia and Adam and all three of us were in a very gay mood, what with the prospect of more than two weeks vacation and the realization that we'd be seeing the family and all our old friends. We sang and talked and laughed the miles away. And yet, I had a few solemn moments, too, when I got to thinking about the change three months had made in me. On my way to college in September, I'd been full of anxieties and uncertainties about the different life and the new acquaintances that lay ahead. Now I felt older and infinitely more sure of myself, confident of my capacity to adjust to new ways and new surroundings. It was as though at that time maturity had been a new garment in which I felt lost and uneasy. Now it fitted me better and I was able to take it for granted.

Some of this inner self-confidence must have been apparent to others as well. Because that night at dinner, as we lingered over dessert, my mother remarked, "You seem more grown up every time you come home, Tobey, more poised and assured."

"I'm glad it shows." I smiled at her. "I feel that way."

Dad said, "College is supposed to make young people more independent and capable of thinking for themselves. It seems to be working with you." He added then, his tone teasing, "Pretty soon you won't need us for a thing, except to pay the bills."

"Don't worry," I told him. "I need all of you for a lot more than that. I've been dying to get home and see you."

"Us," Midge queried dryly, "or Brose?"

"Well, him, too," I had to admit. "But I missed all of you. Honest!"

We sat there, gabbing and laughing, for quite a long while, picking up all the threads that had loosened, but never broken, during our months apart. This was the way it should be with families, I felt. None of us ever doubted the others' interest in our affairs. We all felt an urge to catch up on the things that had happened to every one of us. It gave us a sense of being a part of a circle that could expand to include others, or shrink to however few of us happened to be together, without in the least affecting the strong bonds that united us.

"When is Brose getting home?" Mom queried.

"Any time now." I glanced at my watch. "He's flying. His plane was due an hour ago and his folks were driving in to Chicago to meet him. They'll probably get home before too—"

The phone rang and I left my sentence hanging in mid-air as I raced to answer. My heart pounded and there was a quavery little note in my, "Hello?"

A male voice—but that of a much younger male than Brose—asked purposefully, "Is Midge there?"

"Why—yes," I managed, swallowing my disappointment. "Just a minute." I called then, "Midge, it's for you."

"Is it Judy?" my sister asked as she came into the hall.

"A boy," my lips formed the words quietly and I didn't smile, although I had a struggle to keep my face straight.

My sister's eyebrows disappeared under her bangs in astonishment as she reached for the phone. Instead of being obnoxious and hanging around to listen, I went out to the kitchen where Mom was beginning to stack the dishes in the new dishwasher she'd got for her birthday.

"It was a boy," I told her, "for Midge."

"A boy!" my father exclaimed as he came through the doorway with a stack of dessert plates. "Don't tell me that's starting now with Midge!"

"Poor Henry!" Mom said, smiling at him. "Four daughters are almost too much for one man to cope with, aren't they?"

"I wouldn't say that," Dad demurred, setting his burden on the end of the sink with a clatter. "But it has been kind of peaceful around here since Tobey's been at college. And surely Midge is too young to get interested in boys."

"Don't count on it," my mother said drily. "They seem to start dating younger than they used to, although Midge hasn't actually had a date yet. And of course—" she broke off abruptly at the sound of approaching footsteps.

My sister came slowly into the kitchen. She seemed to be in a trance. Her eyes were wide and shining and her lips just slightly parted, as though something so wonderful had happened, she hadn't quite been able to catch her breath. "It was Kirby," she murmured in a small, enchanted voice.

"Who?" my father demanded. He has always had trouble keeping the various boys in his daughters' lives sorted out.

"Kirby Carmichael," Midge said, a delighted smile curving her lips. The name rang a bell in my memory. Midge had told me something about Kirby Carmichael when I was home for Thanksgiving, but for the life of me I couldn't remember what. "He asked me—" her voice sort of broke with the wondrous enormity of the news she had to impart—"to go to the Fortnightly Club's Christmas Dance with him."

"How wonderful!" I exclaimed.

"Yes, isn't it?" Mom agreed. But there was just a hint of a frown between her eyes. "I don't believe I know Kirby, do I, dear?"

"Probably not," Midge said. "He lives clear over in that new development near the country club."

"Now wait a minute," Dad said. "Let me get something straight. If he lives near the country club, it's not within walking distance of here, or the junior high. So how will you work that?"

"His mother or father will take us," Midge explained in the patient tone one would use with an unreasonable child. "That's how kids our age always have to do when they date, until the boys get old enough to drive."

"Heaven forbid!" my father exclaimed piously.

Mom gave him a warning look. "Then if you go to the dance with Kirby," she asked Midge, "the only difference will be that his parents will see that you get there and home again instead of us? Is that it?"

"Well," Midge admitted dreamily, "that's not the only difference. Miss Hildegarde discourages pairing off at dancing class, only the Christmas Dance. Then she lets the boys ask whomever they want to dance, unless it's a Ladies' Choice. So if you go with a boy that night, it means you get to dance lots more dances, because naturally if he takes you, that means he likes you well enough to ask you to dance every time."

"Midge," I murmured, having recalled belatedly what she'd told me about Kirby Carmichael at Thanksgiving, "I thought he was mostly interested in Betty Lou. Is that all over?"

Midge nodded, beaming. "I guess so, or he wouldn't have asked me. I know they had a scrap and weren't speaking, but I thought maybe they'd make up. They usually do. Only now I guess it's for keeps."

Just then the phone rang again and this time it was Brose. His voice sounded deeper than I had remembered and I got so choked up I could hardly speak for a minute. After our preliminary greetings and a bit of slightly stilted chit-chat, Brose said, "I'll have to stay home for a little while, but how about my dropping by around eight-thirty? I'm sure I can get the car. Maybe we could stop in at Joe's for a hamburger or something?"

"Sounds fine," I agreed.

The queerest sensation gripped me as I hung up a minute later. I felt as though I'd been talking to a stranger, no one I knew at all. But it was Brose, I reminded myself. And certainly I knew him. When we were together the feeling of strangeness and unfamiliarity would fade.

I told my parents I'd be going out for a while with Brose. And I added that I thought I'd take a quick shower, as I was feeling a bit travel-worn after the drive from college. When I went into my bedroom to dress half an hour later, Midge was sitting on the foot of my bed waiting for me.

"Tobey," she began, her expression positively conspiratorial, "you know what you told me when you were home before, about being natural and friendly with the boys and interested in what they're interested in and not thinking about myself so much?" She paused just long enough for my agreeing nod, then plunged on, "Well, it works! It worked on Kirby just like magic. Gee, Tobey, you're wonderful!"

"Well, thanks," I smiled. "But you mean Kirby's the only one you tried it out on?"

"Oh, no," Midge shook her head, so that her pony tail wagged back and forth. "I've been that way to all the boys I know, even ol' Bob Pierson. But when Kirby and Betty Lou had their scrap—well, he seemed to want someone to talk to and naturally I listened, because that's what he was most interested in and I don't happen to like Betty Lou very well, either—she's such a stuck-up."

"I hope you didn't talk about her," I told Midge, as I started getting into my clothes. "I hate gossip."

"No," Midge said, "I didn't say anything mean about her. But it's smart to be a good listener, isn't it? All the advice columns in the papers say so."

"Well, yes," I agreed.

"All I did besides listen," my sister went on, "was to—well, when he was sounding off about how he wasn't going to ask Betty Lou to the Christmas Dance because she'd been such a stinker to him—well, I just sort of dropped a teensy little hint that he could make her even madder if he asked someone else. But that was a couple of days ago," Midge admitted, "so I figured he hadn't even got the idea I was trying to put over— only I guess he did." She smiled dreamily.

"Machiavelli," I teased.

"Mack who?" Midge asked blankly.

"He was an Italian statesman," I explained, "who was given to very devious schemes and plots. Machiavelli."

"Oh." Midge grinned, getting it.

"There's just one thing," I told her. "What if Betty Lou and Kirby make up before the big night?"

"I don't think there's much chance. It's only three days off and he's awful mad at her. Anyway," Midge asked solemnly, "how could he get out of taking me now that he's asked me?"

I smiled at her. "I don't suppose he could very well."

"It's not that I'm so fond of him," Midge said frankly, "although he's a pretty big wheel around junior high. But if I didn't go with him, I'd just have to get taken by my own parents and that's such kid stuff for the Christmas Dance."

I nodded. I understood her feeling perfectly.

Midge wandered downstairs to watch a favorite television program and I finished dressing. I chose a soft blue sweater and a woolen skirt that matched it exactly, then clasped a copper pendant around my neck and stood back to study the effect critically. I couldn't help thinking that it was pretty good.

When the doorbell rang and I heard Brose's voice, my instinct was to hurry down. But I managed to restrain the urge for a few minutes, just so he wouldn't get the idea I was too anxious. As I came down the stairs, he was talking with my parents and Midge in the living room. Had his hair always been so dark and crisp, I asked myself? His shoulders looked wider than usual in his belted trench coat, the collar of which was turned up negligently. Maybe it was partly because Dave was rather short that Brose seemed suddenly so tall.

He turned and grinned at me as I came through the doorway and my heart, which had been beating fast before, pounded harder than ever. "Hi, Tobey."

"Hi, Brose."

He reached out and took my hand for a moment, then let it go. His fingers felt cold.

"Did you—have a good flight?"

"Swell," Brose said. "Real smooth."

"His plane was on time to the minute," Mom contributed to the rather halting conversation. "He was just telling us when you came down."

"Doesn't always happen this time of year." My father did his share.

"No, I guess I was lucky," Brose agreed.

For the life of me, I couldn't think of a thing to say. Mom inquired how he liked college and as Brose answered, I felt a surge of thankfulness that my family had been around when he and I met again. If they hadn't, I thought a trifle wildly, we simply might have stood, looking blankly at each other, unable to summon words to our lips, even the most stilted uninspired words. *Hi, Tobey. Hi, Brose. Did you have a good flight?* What brilliant dialogue!

There was a sharp ache of disappointment in my throat. What did this tall, attractive stranger and I have in common? For three months neither of us had had any part in the things that had happened to the other. Even our association before that seemed blurred and indistinct in my memory. This just couldn't be the Brose I knew so well and used to wrap so easily around my little finger. For all the sense of closeness I felt with him, this might have been our first meeting. What was wrong, I wondered?

"Well, shall we go?" Brose asked.

I nodded and moved dumbly toward the hall closet. He held my coat for me politely, talking casually all the while with my parents, who hovered in the living-room door.

"I won't be very late," I murmured, my voice a bit unsteady. And we both said good night to Midge and Mom and Dad.

The door closed behind us. The night was very cold and clear, with millions of stars overhead. And here I was, walking out into it with an utter stranger.

sixteen

Midge Has a Problem

"ISN'T IT A LOVELY NIGHT?" I BABBLED, AS WE WALKED over to the Gilmans' car parked on our drive. I had to say something!

"Sure is," Brose agreed.

He helped me in, then went around and slid in under the steering wheel. But instead of turning on the ignition, he reached over and put his arms around me, close and hard. And, as if it were the most natural thing in the world, our lips met and clung for a moment. I had not, I realized as my heart hurried and my breath caught in my throat, been thoroughly kissed since that day in the station phone booth when Brose went away. And I liked it. I liked it very much!

"That's better," Brose said, his voice a trifle husky. "Now I know you're Tobey Heydon and not some glamorous, self-assured stranger, who's bent on acting as if we'd never met before."

"You were the one who acted that way," I accused him, laughter bubbling up in my voice. "You scared me to death! I thought college had changed you into a completely different person."

"Not I," Brose denied, chuckling too, his arm still

around my shoulders, holding me close. "You're the one who seemed different, so poised and detached and beautiful."

"Oh, so I used to be homely," I teased.

"No," Brose denied, "you were always pretty. But I guess I just wasn't prepared to have you burst on me without warning that way. It made me all tongue-tied and weak-kneed."

"The exact effect you had on me," I told him.

"I was sure you couldn't possibly care a hoot about me any more," Brose admitted. "That had me worried."

"I thought you'd outgrown me."

Brose pulled me closer and rubbed his cheek against my hair. "You were wrong."

"So were you," I murmured.

Funny what a few months apart could do to two people, who should have known each other far too well to be so silly.

"It was all those girls I knew you must be dating," I told him. "Jan Shelby and the others. I was afraid you'd found someone you liked more than me."

"How do you think I feel about Larry and Dave and Ted, those jerks whose names keep cropping up in your letters?"

"Jealous, I hope," I admitted. "The same way I feel about Jan. Not that I don't want you to date other girls. But I hope you'll go on liking me best."

"You haven't," Brose assured me with a little squeeze, "a thing in the world to worry about."

"You haven't, either," I told him.

It seemed only fair to give him the same assurance he'd given me. And I meant it. Dave and Larry and the others I'd met were good friends, Dave rather closer than the others. But no one else made me feel as Brose did. Warmly happy, easy and excited at the same time. It was wonderful!

We drove around for a while, past some of our favorite landmarks— Then we stopped in at Joe's Grill and it was like Old Home Week. Joe himself shook hands with us, welcoming us back. His dark Grecian features seemed lit from within by the pleasure he felt in having so many of his old customers home again. The place was crowded with our friends who were scattered among the younger high school kids. They seemed to regard us with mingled respect and just a touch of resentment. But we didn't care. Barb and Brose and I and half a dozen others squeezed into the biggest booth and talked our heads off. We laughed and interrupted each other, trying to catch up on all the things that had happened since we'd gone our separate ways. The din was deafening. The juke box blared. It was just as it used to be, and yet there was a subtle difference. No longer were we held together by tight ties of interest and shared activities. The ties had loosened now, our outlooks had widened, yet because of the past we clung together. And if, under our happiness there was a little ache of regret for something young and lost that we could never quite share again, we all ignored it. That, I supposed, was a part of growing up. . . .

It was heavenly to be home again, to sleep as late as I liked in the morning, to have breakfast in my robe in the kitchen, to help a little around the house, to get close to Mom and Dad and Midge all over again. The phone rang incessantly. Brose and I were seeing a lot of each other, we skated together and went for hikes and to the movies, or, when he could get the car, rode

around to see our friends. Everything was the same between us as it had always been. That was one relationship that hadn't changed, unless to grow stronger and
more sure.

"How can you be such fun to be with," I asked him
once, "when you write such horrible letters?"

"Aren't they awful?" he agreed good-naturedly. "But
when I get a pen in my hand my mind goes blank. I
can't help it."

"Suz Herrick's like that, too, about writing letters,"
I told him. "Lucky you aren't writing to her. My letters
are long enough for both of us, I guess."

I had told Brose about Suz and Marilyn and the other
Thetas, as well as about the men I'd dated. And he
had told me a lot about his life at school. Instead of
Jan Shelby being a little blonde, as I'd imagined her,
she was a tall redhead from Texas. But she sounded
attractive, nonetheless, although from the way Brose
spoke of their friendship, I decided it must be quite a
lot like Dave's and mine.

"You don't have to worry about Jan." Brose grinned
at me. "I told her all about you."

"And what did she say?" I queried.

"She said," Brose chuckled, "in that inimitable Texas
drawl of hers, that you sounded like a right nice person.
You'd like Jan."

I wasn't entirely sure he was right, but I didn't argue
the point.

On Friday morning, the day of the Fortnightly Dance,
the phone rang and when I answered it, I recognized
Kirby Carmichael's voice. I called Midge and ambled
into the library, an unreasonable little clutch of fear at

my heart. Why should he be calling her, I wondered? And I didn't make too great an effort not to overhear her end of the short conversation.

This consisted of an inquiring, "Hello?", a pleased, "Oh, yeah," and then a long silence during which Kirby must have talked steadily for a minute or longer. Next Midge's voice, which sounded rather different to me now, muttered, "Well, yes, I guess so." Another pause and then, "Well, yes, sure." Quite a long pause followed, during which Midge listened to what Kirby was saying and I just listened, period. Then my sister said, "It's okay. 'Bye," and hung up.

I went out into the hall, frowning. "Now what was that all about—" I began and then I stopped, staring at Midge, sympathy welling up in me. She was crying quietly, the tears running down her cheeks, her chin unsteady. "Honey," I went to her swiftly, put my arm around her, "what's wrong? What happened?"

"He made up with Betty Lou," Midge sobbed. "And now he's going to take her to the dance instead of me, because he'd already asked her when they had their scrap and now he's afraid if he takes me she'll get mad at him all over again." The last words came out in a heartbroken wail.

"What a little monster!" I exclaimed, hugging Midge harder. "How could he do such a thing after he'd already asked you? How could his parents let him?"

"I don't know." Midge gulped. "I h-hate him. And I hate Betty Lou, too. I'll bet she only made up with him because she heard he was g-going to take me and she didn't want him to."

I imagined she might be quite right. But it wasn't going to help any to let her keep dwelling on that angle of it. I realized that the two of us were alone in the house. Mom had gone out to do some shopping and Dad, of course, was at work. So that meant that I was the only source of comfort and consolation the poor kid had at hand. I tried hard to figure which approach to the problem would do her the most good.

"Maybe so," I agreed soothingly. "But kids who'd act that way aren't worth wasting your tears on. I'm real proud of you, though, for not crying till after you'd hung up, not letting him know how hurt you were."

"I didn't, did I?" Midge sounded a shade less desolate. "I just let him talk and then I said 'okay.' "

"That's right," I agreed. "I heard you. Your attitude was very mature. He's the one who's acting like a little brat."

Midge drew a deep shaken breath and rubbed at her eyes with the back of her hand. "But what am I going to do, Tobey?" she asked. "Judy knows he was going to take me, some of the other kids, too. What'll I tell them?"

"Judy's your friend," I reminded her. "She'll think he's a stinker, too, for treating you this way. I wouldn't say anything to the others. Let them figure things out for themselves. In the excitement of the dance and all, I doubt anyone will pay too much attention to who's with whom and all that. If they do and if they ask you any questions, I'd just say airily that he and Betty Lou made up. And act as if it doesn't make the slightest difference to you, that's the important thing."

"B-but it does," Midge said piteously. "Now my own parents will have to take me."

"You won't be the only one," I reminded her. And I talked on, gradually changing the subject over from

Kirby to Midge's darling new dress and the way she was
going to do her hair for the dance. I even offered to help
her set her pin curls in a special way.

When Mom got home from her shopping, I waylaid
her in the kitchen and told her what had happened.
Midge was on the phone just then, unburdening herself
to Judy. Mom agreed with me that the best course was
to keep Midge's mind off her grievance as much as possible.

"Do you suppose this will help?" Mom asked, fishing
in one of her grocery bags. She brought out a darling
little gardenia corsage in a green florist's box. "I picked
this up because I was afraid Kirby might not think of
one—boys that age are so unpredictable."

"Sure it will," I smiled. "Midge will be tickled pink
with it."

And she was. But even with Mom and me doing our
best to keep things happy and gay, there were gloomy
intervals every now and then as the day wore on. On
the whole, though, Midge was a pretty good scout. As
for myself, I hoped I'd never see Kirby Carmichael. The
temptation to wring his neck might be too great.

In mid-afternoon Midge discovered that she had a
library book that was overdue, so she left to return it,
tying a scarf carefully over her pin curls in order not to
disturb them. She wasn't gone very long and to Mom's
and my relief, she came in looking a little less glum than
she had when she left.

"Guess what," she said. And then, without waiting for
an answer, she rushed on, "I met ol' Bob Pierson at the
library and he walked part way home with me. We got
to talking about the dance tonight and he asked if he
and his folks couldn't pick me up. So I said okay."

Mom and I exchanged a delighted look. This seemed just as real a date as the one with Kirby had been. And while Bob might not be as exciting to Midge, he was certainly more dependable.

"How nice!" Mom and I exclaimed in chorus.

"Yeah," Midge agreed. "It's not that I care anything about Bob. But only drips go to the Christmas Dance by themselves. Anybody's better than nobody."

With this parting word of philosophy, she went over to the phone to call Judy and tell her the news.

That evening, just as we sat down to dinner, the doorbell rang. My father answered it and he came back into the dining-room with a small florist's box in his hand. "For you, Midge," he told her, obviously as curious as the rest of us were as to who would be sending Midge a corsage.

Inside the box, nested in green paper, was a cluster of two gardenias, the exact twin of the corsage Mom had bought earlier. We all craned our necks as Midge tore open the little white envelope that accompanied the flowers.

"It's from Kirby!" she exclaimed in shocked incredulity. "The card says, 'With my apologies.'"

"His parents probably made him do it," Dad guessed.

And Mom nodded. "I imagine they're ashamed of the way he's acted, but don't know just what they can do about it."

"I'd know what I could do—" my father began grimly.

But Midge interrupted, her face set in lines of grievous indecision. "But what'll I do?" she demanded. "I wouldn't wear his old corsage for anything. But the one Mom got me looks just like it and he'll think—" she broke off appalled.

No one could offer any very helpful suggestion. The consensus was that Midge would simply have to go to the dance corsageless, since it was now too late to buy her more flowers of a different variety. After dinner we all sat around sort of on pins and needles while Midge took her shower. I went up to her room to help fix her hair and zip her into her pale blue party dress, which looked lovely on her and was, as Midge wishfully insisted, "practically a formal, only with sleeves."

"A corsage would look so pretty right there," Midge touched her shoulder. "Darn ol' Kirby Carmichael anyway!"

I offered what consolation I could and we went downstairs, where our parents exclaimed over how nice Midge looked. Her hair, thank heavens, had curled just right, soft and natural looking. I didn't think I could have borne it otherwise.

"I better be all ready," Midge said, getting her coat from the closet. "They'll probably just honk for me."

But at that moment the doorbell rang and Mom whispered to Midge with a little hug, "See, you did Bob an injustice."

My father let him in and I was amazed at how well he looked in his gray tweed topcoat and the knife-creased dark blue trousers showing underneath. The only other times I'd seen him, he'd been in jeans and a tee-shirt. His unruly brown hair had been slicked down with a firm hand and his ears were quite pink, with cold or embarrassment, I wasn't sure which.

"Hi, Midge," he said, thrusting a florist's box at her.

"Hi," Midge managed to say, looking blankly from Bob's well-scrubbed face to his unexpected gift. It was quite obvious that she was impressed, as she muttered, "Thanks."

"You're welcome."

We all stood around watching as she opened the box. If it was gardenias, I thought, I would simply curl up and die. But it wasn't. I breathed again and I expect my parents were sharing my sensations as Midge lifted a corsage of pink rosebuds and held it against the shoulder of her blue dress, where it looked quite perfect. "Gee, thanks, Bob," she said again, her voice warming with pleasure. "You didn't have to do that."

"It's okay," Bob said uncomfortably. Then, all in the same breath, "Let's get going. My Dad's waiting."

When the door had closed behind them and we heard the Piersons' car drive off, we just stood there, the three of us, smiling foolishly at each other. Somehow there didn't seem to be anything to say, not for a minute or two, until we were sure our voices would come out steady and not all churned up with happy sentimentality.

Later that evening, when Brose and I were driving over to a party at Kay Lamb's house, I told him all about the events of the day and their satisfactory outcome. "Were we ever that young?" I wondered aloud, a faint smile curling my mouth.

"Sure." Brose chuckled reminiscently. "Only I didn't have the nerve to ask you to any dances when I was Bob's age. I was too chicken."

"I must tell Midge you said that," I laughed. "Maybe there's some hope for poor old Bob after all."

seventeen

Happy Holidays

CHRISTMAS COULDN'T HAVE BEEN MORE PERFECT. THERE was a powdery touch of new snow during the night to cover the world with white magic. We had a big family dinner, with Adam's father and his aunt Tess included. And although my older sister Janet and her family couldn't be with us, we did the next best thing and talked to them in California by long-distance.

I got practically everything I'd hoped for in the way of gifts, mostly clothes, naturally. Brose gave me a darling silver identification bracelet and I gave him one, too. This wasn't really a coincidence. We'd decided ahead of time that this was what we'd do. "Just to remind us who we really belong to, when we're apart," was the way Brose put it. And deep down inside, that was the way I felt, too.

"Do you remember," I asked Brose rather sentimentally when he dropped over late in the afternoon and we went for a long walk, "the Christmas when your mother thought a book would be the perfect thing for you to give me? But you got around her by tucking in a bottle of My Sin perfume and a real dark lipstick."

"I sure do," Brose chuckled. "That was the year

Adam's father made him fill in as Santa Claus at the store and Alicia persuaded the poor guy to come and make a personal appearance for Midge and your sister Janet's kid."

"And then Janet's husband got home unexpectedly from Central America and saw Adam climbing up to the window and mistook him for a burglar—" I broke off and we both dissolved into laughter.

Christmas is a time for reminiscences and Brose and I shared so many memories, some funny, some sad, some embarrassing. Brose could remember when I'd been so young Mom didn't want me to use lipstick and I'd had to snitch Janet's or Alicia's. And my freckles had been the bane of my existence. Now it was Midge who was growing up enough to start worrying about her freckles, while mine had practically faded away. And Brose, whom I could remember in grade school when he'd been inches shorter than I, now towered above me, broad-shouldered and good-looking. It made my heart beat faster just to walk along beside him. We'd dated and scrapped and made up again so many times. I'd worn his class ring for a while, until I'd decided such symbols were really a sign of immaturity. We might be in love right now, might marry later on. Happiness surged up in me at the thought. But we wanted to be very sure and there was plenty of time. Whatever the future held for us, though, one thing was certain. Our friendship was a warm, enriching experience for us both. That was enough for now and I was grateful.

As though his thoughts had arrived at the same conclusion that mine had, Brose said, "We're lucky, you know it?"

I nodded. It was so often like that with us. We'd

be thinking the same thoughts, so that only a few words were necessary to make our meaning clear to each other. Almost like mental telepathy, I reflected.

Still Brose apparently felt he had to explain what he meant a little more fully. "All the fun we've had together, the crazy things we've done, the way we understand each other so well—it's a good sound basis for the way we feel. None of this crazy infatuation stuff, where you meet a girl and fall for her hard right then and there. Why, I know you inside out, Tobey, and I like the things I know about you. The way you say what you think and stand up for the things you believe in, the way you're honest, even if it gets you into a jam now and then."

"I like what I know about you, too," I told him. "The way you're so dependable and calm in an emergency, like the night the crowd got marooned out on Gull Island and I was scared silly. And you're so sensible, too, the way you figure things out for yourself instead of just following the mob, whether you agree with them or not."

Brose asked, his voice serious, "You haven't met anyone at college you like better?"

I shook my head. "I've made friends there, of course, just as you have. That was what we planned, wasn't it? But there isn't anyone I'm really crazy about." I found myself then, quite naturally, talking about Dave and Larry and the others. But especially about Dave, because he was the type of person I felt sure Brose would like if they had a chance to know each other. Maybe, I realized, that was partly why I was drawn to Dave, because he was a little like Brose in his attitudes, his outlook on life, his common sense and dependability.

When we got back to my house, it was blue dusk. The living room was dusky, too, lit only by the Christmas tree lights and the dancing glow of the cannel coal in the fireplace. There were fat white candles trimmed with sequins on the mantel and a drift of Christmas boxes, opened now, spilled their contents out, beneath the tree. Everyone was talking and laughing and Brose and I were absorbed into the group in a matter of minutes. My family, thank goodness, has never been the stiff or formal type.

The phone rang and Midge went to answer it. But a moment later her voice called from the hall, "It's for you, Tobey."

Probably Barb, I thought, calling to see what sort of lovely loot I'd acquired. But as I met Midge in the doorway she whispered, "It's a man. I don't know who, though."

Neither did I, certainly. But my curiosity was aroused. "Hello?" I said into the mouthpiece and proceeded to get the surprise of my life.

"Hi, Tobey," a deep, tantalizingly half-familiar voice, with laughter underlying it, spoke. "Remember me? Dick Allen."

"Dick?" I gasped incredulously. "But—where are you?"

"Home," he said. "Right here in little old Edgewood. I got ten days leave and just flew in this morning from points south. Even surprised the family, because I wasn't sure I could make it till the last minute and I didn't want to get their hopes up."

There was so much to talk about, so many things to catch up on. When I slipped back into the living room some fifteen minutes later, I was conscious of Brose's

"He sounds like a good joe," Brose admitted
tone was so grudging, we both had to laugh.

"If you want to know," I informed Brose, "tł
just one way in which you don't appeal to me."

"How?" Brose sounded a little anxious.

"You write such horrible letters," I sighed.

"I know," Brose admitted. "But, honestly, I
Tobey. It's just that I hate to write."

I smiled up at him, feeling a touch of sympatł
"Would you rather not write at all, since it comes
hard for you?"

"Gee!" he exclaimed, his face lighting. "You mea
that would be all right with you?"

He sounded so hopeful, I didn't have the heart to holc
out. "We could try it," I suggested, "and see how it
goes. Oh, if there's anything vital that either of us wants
the other to know, we could send off a letter, of course.
But you'd be happier if we didn't try to keep up a
regular correspondence, wouldn't you?"

"Well, yes," Brose admitted, "although I like to hear
from you. But I sure hate to answer. And you know how
I feel about you, don't you, Tobey?" He caught my hand
in his and held it tight. "But I can't put it on paper,
so there's no use trying."

"You're just afraid I'll blackmail you," I teased, and
we both laughed. "But I'll agree to not writing on one
condition."

"What's that?"

"Promise to let me know if you change your mind
about liking me best."

"Then you won't be hearing from me," Brose said
seriously, "because I never expect to change my mind
about that."

questioning frown. But there was no use trying to cover up. He'd learn Dick was home soon enough, whether I told him or not. News like that travels fast. So I just came out with it flatly, "Dick's home!"

There was a murmur of surprise and pleasure all about. My family knows the Allens well and we all like Dick. But Brose's tone did not reflect the general delight as he muttered, "I thought he was in Panama."

There was no question but that Brose, at least, would have been perfectly content to have him stay there.

The rest of the holidays moved past in a happy rush, so far as I was concerned. If there is anything that contributes more to a girl's good time on her Christmas vacation than one devoted man, it is two devoted men. And while Dick might not be as devoted as Brose, he certainly lavished a good deal of his time and attention on me and I couldn't deny that I loved it. Dick, deeply tanned from his months in the tropics, debonaire and full of fun as always, and more handsome than ever in his navy uniform, was not someone to be lightly brushed aside. Besides, it wouldn't have been patriotic to treat a home-on-leave service man so inconsiderately.

Dick and I were good friends, nothing more. We both knew that and I tried to make Brose see it that way, too. But he had never been too reasonable where Dick was concerned. And certainly Dick did nothing to keep from rubbing him entirely the wrong way whenever they were together.

"I think you like making Brose see red," I accused Dick once. "You go out of your way to antagonize him."

"Sure, I do," Dick admitted, grinning. "Let me have that much satisfaction, anyway. He's got the girl I want.

Isn't that enough for him, without me being agreeable, too?"

"You, with a girl in every port," I kidded him. "You don't really want to add me to your collection. I'm just someone you like to look up when you get home, and forget as soon as you sail away again."

"Have it your way." Dick's eyes held a lazy tantalizing gleam. It was so hard to tell when he was serious or when he was handing you a line. Sometimes I doubted whether he knew himself. "Trample on my poor busted heart if you want to."

I laughed at him. "If your heart's busted, someone else did the dastardly deed, not I. Probably it was some sultry Spanish beauty with a rose between her teeth."

"You mean Conchita Juanita Lolita Pepita Lopez down Mehico way?" Dick asked.

We always had fun together. Dick dropped over to our house almost every day. Sometimes he'd come when Brose was there and then Brose would sit glaring at him.

Once I told Brose, "Honestly, I think he acts the way he does partly to tease you. If you didn't get so mad—"

"Sometime," Brose interrupted darkly, "I'll clobber him."

"Now wouldn't that be silly?" I asked.

"He's spoiling my whole vacation," Brose growled.

"I've gone out with you a dozen times," I pointed out, "to once or twice with Dick. I can't help it if he comes over to see me sometimes."

"I'm not sure you want to help it," Brose argued.

But we didn't have a real scrap, although we got right to the verge of one a couple of times. The trouble was, I could see things from Brose's viewpoint when I tried. Probably, in his place, I'd have been mad at Dick, too.

But in my place it was all fun and the holiday sped past much too quickly.

We had a big New Year's Eve party at our house, two parties in fact. I had a crowd of my friends over and my parents had some of their cronies in for bridge. But the young crowd took over the living room, where we could dance to the record player, while the older one staked out the library. Not that we all stayed put. Some of us kept gravitating back and forth from one group to the other, keeping things delightfully stirred up. It's amazing how much fun you can have with older people, once you get over the hurdle of considering them fuddy-duddies. Midge had gone to a slumber party at one of her girl friend's, so we didn't have to cope with a crowd quite as young as hers.

At midnight Brose gave me a big kiss and we all held hands and sang Auld Lang Syne. There was quite a bit of kissing going on, as the whistles and noisemakers shrilled out a welcome to the new year. I saw Dick kissing Barb and they both seemed to be enjoying it, but I didn't feel the slightest qualm of jealousy. In fact, it struck me that it would be nice if they should get interested in each other.

Brose flew back to Colorado two days later. His folks drove him in to the city to get his plane, but I couldn't go along, since their car was full of the relatives who were visiting them. So Brose and I said our good-byes the night before, when we had our last date. I felt quite tearful as I made my way upstairs to bed. The realization that I wouldn't be seeing him for five whole months lay like a heavy hand on my heart. And this time I wouldn't be hearing from him, either.

At the last minute, Dick decided to go up to college

with Alicia and Adam and me. Of course, I didn't mind. It was easy to understand why he wanted to go. After all, Central was his old school and he still had lots of friends there. He wasn't going merely on my account, I felt sure. Just the same I was glad that the idea hadn't struck him until Brose had gone. I could just imagine his reaction.

For three days Dick stayed at his fraternity house and looked up all his old friends, both male and female. But he didn't seem as interested in any other girl as he did in me. And I'd have been less than human not to get a big bang out of his attentions. My sister Thetas were green-eyed with envy. "All that and a uniform, too," Marilyn put it with an exaggerated sigh. "Honestly, some people get all the breaks." She smiled as she said it. Her sense of humor, as well as her disposition, seemed to have improved under the influence of the Thetas.

Whenever Dick took me to the Barn, I felt a glow of pride at all the admiring looks he drew. Even if my interest in him wasn't a bit romantic, our association had undoubtedly added to my prestige. And both Dave and Larry were outspoken in their resentment of him, which was quite flattering. Part of the time Dick handed me a line which I knew darned well could only have grown so smooth with constant practice. But sometimes he was almost brotherly in the advice he gave me. After he had met both Dave and Larry, he informed me that Larry, in his opinion, was a junior-grade wolf. Dick liked Dave much better.

"You know what?" he asked one evening as we walked back to the Theta house across the moonlit campus. "Dave is a lot like Brose in some ways."

"I know," I admitted. "That occurred to me, too."

"I have to admit they're not bad guys," Dick went on, "even if they are my deadly rivals. In fact, I shouldn't be surprised if they'd both make very good husbands. But since bigamy is frowned on, why not settle for me instead?"

"If I said 'yes' you'd be horrified." I laughed. "You know you haven't any plans for settling down."

"I know it," Dick said. "But I figure I'm on safe ground with you, because you have no such plans, either. Right?"

"Right," I agreed.

Before I was through college, I suspected, Dick would have fallen in love and married someone else. The thought didn't carry any hurt at all. I liked him too well not to want him to be happy. And that, I imagined, was exactly the way he felt about me.

eighteen

Poor Suz

WITH DICK'S DEPARTURE, LIFE SETTLED DOWN TO NORMAL, if you can call mid-semester exams normal. However, I did rather better with these than I expected, proving that studying pays. And right on the heels of mid-semesters, like a wonderful dessert following a meal you hadn't liked too well, came the thrill and excitement of my formal initiation into the Thetas. The candle-lit ceremony, hushed and dignified, with all the actives and pledges in white evening dresses, was quite impressive. It effectively blurred the less happy recollection of some of the silly stunts we pledges had to do before the final ceremony, such as going to class with our clothes on backward and not speaking to anyone but our teachers for twenty-four endless hours. Still, it was worth it, I felt, to be a full-fledged Theta at last.

For some reason I didn't entirely understand, I was having more dates now. Every week end was filled with activity of one sort or another. Often I went out with Dave, occasionally with Larry or with some of the other boys I'd met.

" 'Them as has, gits,' " Suz Herrick quoted wistfully one afternoon as we walked toward her dorm to pick up my sterling qualities and not care about my looks. What I didn't count on was that I might meet him now."

"Tell me," I said.

The real sympathy I felt must have sounded in my tone, because Suz unburdened herself completely. It seemed she had an instructor in chemistry named Dennis Bishop, not a full professor, one who was much younger than the general run of teachers. A graduate student, he was working on his master's degree and, according to Suz, was quite a person.

"It's so crazy," poor Suz admitted, "that he should affect me this way and still not even know I'm alive. And he doesn't, I'm sure, except that he might find my face vaguely familiar if we happened to see each other outside of lab."

She talked on and on about him. I felt a bit like the innocent bystander who got swept away when the dam burst. But I listened to Suz's confidences and felt so sorry for her that my throat ached and my eyes stung a little. This, I suspected, was the first time she had fallen so hard for someone that she couldn't keep it to herself. Finally, when she was all talked out, she swore me to secrecy, although I wouldn't have dreamed of telling anyone.

When I said as much, Suz apologized. "I know you wouldn't, Tobey. It's just—well, I'd simply die if he ever knew how I felt."

"But if he never knows," I objected, "what can come of it?"

"Nothing," Suz said flatly, all safely locked up in her little cage of self-control again. "I don't expect anything to come of it. Why should anyone so wonderful be interested in me?"

a book she'd offered to loan me. "Remem
fall how you were worrying for fear no on
ask you for a date?"

I nodded, smiling. But some half-sensed n
in her voice made me offer, "If you'd like m
up a blind date any time, Suz—"

"I wasn't hinting," she cut in sharply. Then
softening, "Sorry, Tobey. It's just that blind d₂
do much for a person's ego."

She sounded so low, my heart twisted with p
was such a wonderful person, intelligent, witty, fu
with. She wasn't even bad-looking, yet so far as
she hadn't had a date since she came to college.
was it, I asked myself, that seemed to set some
apart, make them popular with boys, when often
were no prettier than Suz? Was it an inner assu₁
that they were attractive and likable, that sparked
whole personality and drew boys to them? Suz seer
friendly enough with her male classmates, yet they sim₁
didn't think of her when it came to dating. I couldi
figure it out and I knew Suz was too intelligent not
have tried to solve her problem for herself. But evidentl
she hadn't come up with any workable solution. I hac
never really thought she cared before. Now she sounded
sunk and unhappy. I wondered what had happened to
change the situation for her?

We were too close friends for me to feel I couldn't
ask. "You usually seem so philosophical. Is there any
special reason why it's suddenly begun to matter?"

Suz's smile was not quite steady. "You would notice
that," she said. "And you're so right. It does matter
suddenly. I always figured when I was through college
the man I might want would be old enough to appreciate

"That's a very defeatist attitude," I argued. "If something sort of drew you to his attention, he might like you. As it is, you're just one of a crowd of students to him."

"Yes," Suz said in her droll way, "I know. But if you're implying I should chase him like some of these silly girls pursue every unmarried instructor under forty, no, thanks."

"That's not what I meant at all—" I began.

But Suz wouldn't let me finish. She started to talk about something entirely different, apparently considering the subject of Dennis Bishop closed.

I hated to let her problem drop there. I've never been one to keep my nose out of other people's affairs if I feel a bit of meddling might prove helpful. And I liked Suz so well. I wanted her to be happy. Still, I might have figured there was nothing I could do about it, if it hadn't been for one thing. A few days after Suz had unburdened herself, I met Dennis Bishop.

Larry Hartnett and I were standing talking in front of the Science Building, when a quite ordinary-looking young man with close-cropped hair and rather owlish horn-rimmed glasses came out. He stopped to speak briefly with Larry about a chemistry experiment and Larry's casual introduction caused me to do an unobtrusive double-take. Could this, I asked myself incredulously, be the paragon of masculine attractiveness, super-intellect and all-around charm Suz had described in such glowing terms? If so, it could only be the case when he was viewed through Suz's enchanted eyes. Certainly I found him a good deal short of terrific. He seemed pleasant enough and not revoltingly homely. But I couldn't see that he was any more attractive in his masculine way than Suz in her feminine fashion. And why she shouldn't be able to arouse his interest if she tried, I couldn't imagine. The trouble was, I realized, that poor Suz, with her utter lack of wiles and coquetry, would have no idea how to go about trying. What a pity!

After the instructor had gone on his way, Larry offered to buy me a soda at the Barn. It seemed a wonderful chance to pump Larry a bit and find out his opinion of Dennis Bishop. Larry, I learned, had nothing against him. He said Bishop was all right as instructors went and not too hard on his classes. This, coming from Larry, was pretty high praise. "But why are you so interested in him?" he asked curiously.

"Oh, I'm not really," I denied. "It's just—" I tried to think of a reasonable excuse for my questions, "well, he struck me as rather an unusual person."

"He did?" Larry sounded surprised. "Why?"

"I don't know," I hedged. "Maybe just because some of the girls I know talk as if he is. They seem to find him interesting."

"You mean because he isn't married?" Larry chuckled. "Or because he was born in China?"

"Was he?" I ignored Larry's first question. "I didn't know that."

"Sure," Larry answered. "His parents were missionaries. He grew up there and could speak Chinese before he knew English. It is kind of interesting, the things he can tell you about China when he gets started."

"I'll bet," I agreed a shade absently.

My thoughts were racing off in mad pursuit of an idea that had just struck me. Suz did a good deal of feature writing for the *Central Clue*, the college paper. Why shouldn't she do a piece about Dennis Bishop and his unusual background? If I could persuade her to interview him, it would give them a chance to get much better acquainted than they were ever likely to in class. Men always loved to talk about themselves and Suz was a good listener. It might be just the gimmick needed to bring her more personally to the instructor's notice. After that, who knew what might happen?

Naturally, I was anxious to tell Suz all about my brilliant scheme. I rushed through my homework that night in order to drop over to Mercer Hall. But Suz's reaction proved disappointing to say the least.

"I couldn't interview him!" she exclaimed. "I'd just freeze up and my mind would go blank. Besides, he'd suspect that it was simply an excuse for me to get to talk with him—that is, unless we based the article on interviews with several professors."

"Well, do it that way then," I prodded. "Interview as many as it takes to make the article seem right—but interview him, too, Suz. You've got to! It would be a perfect way for you two to get better acquainted. And that's what you want, isn't it?"

"How I'd love to," Suz murmured, her eyes bright with dreams. If only Dennis Bishop could have seen her looking like that! But then she shook her head firmly. "I couldn't do it, though. Not possibly!"

And despite all my arguments, she stuck to her guns. Suz could be very stubborn when she chose. Finally I gave up the whole idea and decided to leave her to cope with her own romantic problems. But a few days later I learned that something had come of my scheme, after all, even if it wasn't exactly the result I'd hoped for.

"You know that article you suggested," Suz broached the subject enthusiastically the next time we ran into each other. "Well, I mentioned it to the editor and he thought it would be a good idea to interview five or six instructors who have especially interesting backgrounds. So I've already arranged four of the interviews and I wondered if you'd do me a big favor?"

"What?" I asked, a slightly dubious note in my voice. My poor little original idea seemed to be snowballing.

"Tobey, will you talk to Dennis Bishop for me?" Suz coaxed.

"Me?" I demanded ungrammatically.

"Please." Suz laid an insistent hand on my arm. "I'll arrange for the time and everything. I do so want him to be a part of the article. But I simply can't go and talk to him, ask him questions. And after all, you thought of it."

"I only dreamed up a way for you to get to know him better," I argued. "If I interview him, it'll defeat the whole purpose."

"Then we'll just have to leave him out," Suz sighed. "I can't do it. He might suspect how I feel and I couldn't risk it."

She sounded so utterly forlorn I felt sorry for her. It annoyed me, though, to think of anyone so generally sensible as Suz getting herself tied up in such emotional knots that it was almost impossible to help her. Still, since the original idea had been mine, I supposed I couldn't let her down now.

"Oh, all right," I agreed grumpily. "Set up the interview and I'll talk to your precious professor. But I still think you're loopy to pass up a chance like this."

Suz was overwhelmingly grateful. In fact, I felt a shade ashamed of myself as she thanked me over and over. Because already, far back in my mind, the tiny light of a terrific idea had begun to glow like a little candle, brightening the dark.

nineteen

A Little Like Fate

WHENEVER I GOT TO THINKING ABOUT BROSE, WHICH WAS quite often, a queer little ache of emptiness settled around my heart. Even his short unsatisfactory letters had been better than no letters at all. I realized that now, but I'd agreed to our not writing, so I wouldn't back down. He sent me a dozen red roses for Valentine's Day, and a card with "Love" scrawled across it. I took that as meaning that everything was the same between us. But that didn't stop me from wondering what he was doing, whether he missed me, whom he was dating now, all sorts of troubling questions. Sometimes my imagination would get so stirred up I could hardly bear it. But then common sense would come to my rescue. After all, we'd promised to write if either of us got vitally attracted to anyone else. So no news was good news.

My knowledge of Suz's secret interest in Dennis Bishop made me especially susceptible to thoughts of Brose. It seemed to me that Suz and her instructor might be very congenial if they just got better acquainted. Their tastes and ideas might be as much alike as Brose's and mine were. They might really fall in love. Suz would make a wonderful wife for a college professor. Maybe she'd ask me to be a bridesmaid at their wedding. At this point in my rosy reflections I was brought up short by the memory that it was I, not Suz, who was going to interview Dennis Bishop for the *Clue*, I who would listen to his stories of China. How could that further his interest in Suz, I asked myself disgustedly? And the answer was, it couldn't. Nothing would come of it, nothing at all, unless I had the nerve to go through with the crazy scheme that kept floating around in my mind.

On a bleak March morning Suz told me she had set up my interview for four-thirty that afternoon. "He'll be expecting you in the lab right after his last class," she explained. Her cheeks were quite pink with vicarious excitement and her eyes shone. I'd never seen her look so pretty. "And really try to draw him out, will you, Tobey?" she went on. "He's sort of quiet."

"I'll do my best," I said, "but you know this sort of thing isn't my line. Why don't you come with me? Then you could make suggestions, or at least lend me moral support."

But Suz shook her head, apparently scared to death at the mere idea. "I'll wait in my room," she told me. "Bring your notes straight there as soon as you finish, so I can write them up."

So that was the way we left it. During my afternoon classes I'm afraid my thoughts wandered pretty far afield from the subjects at hand. Should I, or shouldn't I? And if I did, could I get away with it?

I still hadn't made up my mind as I left my last class. Even with the chill wind thrusting at my back, my footsteps dragged, slowed by the indecision that gripped me. Then Jean Clyde caught up with me. And as I answered her casual greeting, our encounter seemed like such a definite gesture on the part of Fate that I determined to take the plunge and see what happened.

I stumbled just a little and shut my eyes, putting out one hand to steady myself on the trunk of a tree we happened to be passing.

"What's the matter?" Jean's voice was concerned.

"How—funny," I said hesitantly. "Suddenly I feel—sort of faint."

"Faint?" Jean frowned and took my arm.

"Dizzy," I elaborated, shutting my eyes again and swaying a little, so that Jean could feel I was leaning on her.

"For Heaven's sake!" she exclaimed, sounding so alarmed that I felt a small qualm of guilt squirm in me. But I couldn't turn back now. She gasped, "What can I do?"

"Maybe—" my voice was only a shaken breath above a whisper, "if you could help me over to the Infirmary—"

Fortunately it was the next building along the street. I'd noticed that before I started. Leaning on Jean's arm, I managed to make it, tottering realistically. Dr. Matthews was just coming out of her office as we entered the hall and Jean turned me over to her worriedly.

"She just got dizzy," Jean explained.

"Light-headed," I elaborated, as Dr. Matthews eased me down into a chair beside her desk. "Nothing serious —just feel sort of woozy—" my voice trailed off. Then suddenly I leaned forward a little, putting my hand to my head. "Oh, Jean—would you do something for me right away? I had an appointment to interview someone for Suz Herrick—for the *Clue*, you know? She'll be in her room—if you'll just get hold of her she can take care of it."

"Well, sure," Jean said, backing toward the door as Dr. Matthews unbuttoned my blouse and started using her stethoscope. "Sure, Tobey. I'll go tell her and then come back and see how you are. You don't think," she asked the doctor, "it's anything serious?"

"We'll see," Dr. Matthews said.

I felt guiltier and guiltier as the doctor listened to my heart, took my pulse and temperature, asked me questions. Had I been dieting? No. Was my stomach upset? Well, no. Had I ever fainted? No, never. Finally, I couldn't bear it any longer.

"I—I feel much better now," I told her. "In fact, I feel perfectly all right."

The doctor leaned back and fixed me with a stern eye, before which I felt myself shrivel slightly. "Are you sure you didn't feel perfectly all right when you came in here?"

I scrunched down a little further in my chair, trying to fix my eyes on the rows of bottles in the glass-fronted cabinet behind Dr. Matthews, rather than on her accusing face. But I liked her too well to go on deceiving her. "I—wasn't really sick at all," I admitted, looking at her again.

Her clear gaze softened a little, but her voice held a note of disappointment, as she asked, "Were you trying to get out of a test or something?"

"No," I denied quickly. "No, it wasn't anything like that." It seemed the most natural thing in the world to go on and tell her all about it. After all, Suz's secret would be quite safe with Dr. Matthews. I finished, "I figured if I just called up and told her I was sick, she'd know it was a stall to make her talk to Mr. Bishop herself. But with Jean backing me up, it will sound real authentic. And by this time," I glanced at the clock on the desk, "Suz will be there at the lab, interviewing him. She couldn't do anything else, really, with him expecting someone to come."

"No, I suppose not," Dr. Matthews agreed. A smile pulled at her lips. "And you figure that's all it will take, for them just to talk to each other outside of class?"

"It may not do a bit of good," I had to admit. "But at least she'll be something more to him than just another student in one of his classes. And she likes him so well. It might help for them to be thrown together, don't you think?"

Dr. Matthews pursed her lips thoughtfully. "I suppose it might," she nodded. "At least, it shouldn't do any harm."

"And you won't give me away?" I coaxed.

"Not," the doctor said with a twinkle, "unless you plan to make a regular thing of such phony attacks. After all," she smiled, "how would the shy ones like Suz get along if it weren't for helpful friends like you to do a bit of finagling for them?"

Dr. Matthews is a very understanding woman. . . .

With Jean having spread the word about my dizziness I found my sorority sisters most solicitous when we got back to the Theta House. Try as I would to convince them that I felt perfectly all right now, Jean still argued that she thought the doctor had let me come home too soon. "If you could have seen yourself," she told me in her dramatic way. "You turned so pale I was sure you were going to faint right there on my hands! I was scared silly!"

What an actress I must be, I thought wryly. Either that or Jean's imagination was working overtime. "How did Suz act when you told her?" I asked.

"As though I'd stabbed her in the back." Jean frowned, remembering. "At first she didn't seem to believe you were really sick, but when I told her Dr. Matthews was taking care of you at the Infirmary, that convinced her. So then she started going through all her clothes like a cyclone and mumbling something about having to look her best for some interview. I didn't stay to hear any more. What was it all about anyway?"

"Just a job she wanted me to do for the *Clue*," I explained, "but, of course, I couldn't." I hoped I wasn't blushing.

Everyone advanced a different theory as to what had been wrong with me. Coming down with flu, a touch of indigestion—or maybe, Marilyn felt, I might need glasses. They all treated me with such gentle consideration, I felt guiltier than ever. Even Dave, serving dinner, told me sympathetically he was glad I was feeling well enough to eat.

My sorority sisters made me go right to bed after dinner. It did me no good to argue that Dr. Matthews had said I'd be quite all right. I didn't really mind too much. What with hearing nothing whatever from Suz, I was feeling half sick with curiosity as to what had happened. Whenever the phone rang, I cringed a little inwardly, afraid it was Suz and that she might be angry with me for letting her down.

But Suz didn't phone. Instead she dropped over to the sorority house to see me. As she came into my room, my heart hammered against my ribs and I started to apologize.

But Suz broke in gently, "Tobey, of course it's all right. You couldn't help getting sick. Are you really feeling better?"

"Oh, yes," I said positively, "but—"

"Tobey," Suz broke in again, her tone dreamy, "in a way it seems almost like fate."

"How do you mean?" I asked uncertainly.

"Your getting sick," Suz went on, sitting down on the edge of my bed and looking at me fondly. "Oh, I'm terribly sorry you didn't feel well, but—" she drew a deep breath and her voice came out a note lower, "oh, Tobey, the interview went so well. He's so interesting to talk with, really talk, I mean, not just a lot of routine questions and answers about chemistry experiments."

"You got plenty of material for your article?" I asked, feeling my way carefully.

"Oh, yes," Suz nodded, her eyes bright. "And not only that. It was getting dark by the time we finished, so he walked all the way back to Mercer with me. He—he actually seemed to enjoy being with me, Tobey."

"Why not?" I tried to speak lightly, but there was a little emotional quaver in my voice.

"Oh, well," Suz smiled and shrugged her shoulders just a bit. "Of course, nothing may come of it. But he did mention that some paintings he brought from China are going to be exhibited in Art Hall next week. And he said he wanted to take me to see them and explain them to me. And I said I'd like that."

I had never heard her sound so happy. I had never felt happier myself. If it hadn't been for the fact that I was supposed to have had an inexplicable attack of faintness that afternoon, I would have leaped out of bed and done a few dance steps out of sheer exuberance. As it was, I contended myself with saying merely, "I see what you mean. It does seem a little like fate, doesn't it?"

twenty

Bad News

SPRING DESCENDED ON THE CAMPUS ALMOST OVERNIGHT.
The cherry trees back of the Library burst into a cloud
of lacy white bloom and the soft green of new grass
edged the winding paths. The air smelled good and there
was a sort of exuberant madness bubbling in everyone.
Fraternities serenaded sororities and scarcely an evening
passed that didn't find us hanging out of our windows,
thrilled by wonderful old harmonies like the "Whiffen-
poof Song" and "Across the Wide Missouri." It was
good to be young and alive and we knew it.

Every week end brought some special event. There
was Dad's Day in April and Mother's Day in May, with
banquets and pageants and queens to be crowned. I
got a big bang out of seeing my parents and showing
them the school, having them meet all my friends and
vice versa. I heard from Mom that Midge was getting
along fine, having fun with her crowd, going on bike
hikes and to the movies and being popular enough with
the boys at Fortnightly so that she had got over her fear
of being a wallflower.

"Whatever advice you give her in your letters must
be working," Mom smiled at me. "In fact, you may

not know it but she shares them with several of her close friends. And they all consider you the final authority on any question involving boys."

"Maybe," I said, "I should do a column called, 'How to Get Your Man in Junior High.'"

Mom's and my eyes met in a look of understanding. And I knew that both of us were glad my suggestions to Midge had proved helpful. Growing up isn't the easiest thing in the world. . . .

Spring was the season, too, for a lot of fraternity and sorority dances and I got to go to my share of them. Dave scraped up the money to take me to his fraternity dance. I borrowed a pale blue formal from Jean Clyde for the occasion—a lot of clothes swapping went on around the Theta house!—and Dave thought it most becoming.

"When I'm an old, old man," he told me as we danced, "I'll still remember how you look tonight, in that blue dress and pink corsage and those little sparkly earrings like stars."

"I'll remember how you look, too," I told him.

"In my rented dinner jacket with the sleeves just a little too long," Dave said soulfully, "and my brand new haircut?"

We laughed and the music swirled around us, soft yet insistent. The lights, as was always the case at fraternity dances, were very low and the crowd so thick you could hardly move.

Dave went on, following his train of thought, "I'll tell my grandchildren my date was the prettiest girl here and that she smelled like lilies-of-the-valley and that I was a little bit in love with her, just enough to make the evening exciting."

I smiled and didn't say anything. But I thought I might be a little in love with Dave, too—oh, not for keeps, but just liking him a lot, enjoying the feel of his arm around me as we danced, getting a bang out of his low voice stirring the hair above my ear. Brose wouldn't mind the way I felt, not really, no more than I would mind his dancing close to Jan Shelby from Texas and murmuring sweet nothings into her ear. It didn't mean anything, but it was fun. Impermanent as Dave's and my feeling for each other might be, it was warm and sweet for the moment and that was enough.

The spring days passed in a rush. There were term papers to be written, finals looming darkly ahead. By dint of working reasonably hard all year, I'd maintained the B average which was my goal. I even felt hopeful of an A in English Comp. The thought made me wonder how Brose was doing in his English, without me to help him. The memory of the hours we'd spent doing our homework together filled me with a sharp loneliness for him. As the college year grew closer to its end, my urge to be with Brose grew and strengthened. He haunted my thoughts, crowding out Dave and the other men I dated.

"Sometimes," Dave complained one starry night when he and Baby and I had gone for a long walk, "I get the notion your thoughts are far away. It's enough to make Baby and me jealous."

"Don't your thoughts slip ahead to summer?" I asked him. "It's so near now."

"Sure." Dave said. "I can't really blame you."

"What are you going to do this summer?" I queried. "Just work?"

"If you could call it that," Dave said. "I've got a

regular summer job back home, lifesaver at the town swimming pool. I get a swell tan and have girls buzzing around me like flies. Sometimes I almost feel ashamed to take the money, but I do."

We laughed together. I was glad Dave was going to have a nice vacation, too.

There was a lot of talk about summer plans around the Theta house. Several of the girls were going to Europe, some had summer jobs, others frankly intended to loaf and take life easy. I hadn't quite made up my mind yet, although I might take a job if I could find something not too demanding. But I wanted to have plenty of time for Brose.

"You're pretty gone on the guy, aren't you?" Marilyn asked one night as we lay across our beds, just talking.

"Afraid so," I admitted. But I wasn't really afraid. The deepening realization of how much Brose meant to me filled me with delight, not fear. "How about you?" I asked Marilyn. "Isn't there someone special for you back home?"

She shook her head, a faint smile curving her lips. "There was one I liked a lot in high school, but it wouldn't be the same now. I realized that when I saw him at Christmas time. He thought he was such a big shot in high school and I thought so, too. He drove a red convertible and his father has an important job with General Motors and all the girls chased him. But now—" she shrugged, "well, I guess I just sort of outgrew him. He hasn't changed any, and I have."

"I know you've changed," I told her. "You've grown up a lot this year, your sense of values is different."

She nodded, asking, "Remember how I had my heart so set on the Taus at first?"

I remembered. We could both smile about it now.

"What a dope I was," Marilyn admitted. "My idea of sororities was strictly kid stuff. You and Suz had the right slant all the time. It's the girls in a club that count, not how much they have or what a big splash they make. When I think of all I'd have missed if I hadn't been asked to join the Thetas—" she left it at that.

"The Thetas would have missed a lot, too," I told her.

And it was quite true. Marilyn had a terrific capacity for work when her interest was involved. Her drive and enthusiasm had made the Thetas' project with the Old People's Home a much more comprehensive endeavor than it could have been without her. The sorority had helped direct these latent qualities of hers toward other than purely selfish ends. But, by the same token, we had reaped the benefits of them, too.

Marilyn smiled at me. I felt sure she knew what I meant without my going into detail. We understood each other so much better than we had at first. We liked each other more, too. But you couldn't put such things into words without getting sticky. There was no use trying.

School would be over early in June. By the first of May I was counting the days. Brose lived in my thoughts so constantly it was quite a struggle to concentrate on my studies. I felt sure that he, too, was looking forward eagerly to summer, floating on the same soft pink cloud of anticipation that bore me up.

Then, when only three weeks remained until the end of the term, I was doing my French one evening when someone called from downstairs, "Tobey, quick! Long distance call for you."

My heart did a small flip-flop. Was someone sick at home? Mom and Dad did call occasionally, but usually on a Sunday or some holiday. This was just a plain Monday night.

My feet had raced down the stairs almost as fast as my thoughts had raced from one troubling possibility to another. I held the receiver to my ear and gasped breathlessly, "Hello?"

"Tobey?" The voice, incredibly, was Brose's.

"Yes, Brose." I was torn between delight and fear. "Is anything wrong?"

"Only that I miss you," Brose said. "How are you?"

"Just fine," I told him. "But—isn't this costing you a mint?"

"The rates are less at night," he said, "Anyway, I had to talk to you. There's something I've got to find out."

"What?" I frowned, trying to imagine any question vital enough to warrant a phone call all the way from Colorado.

"Tobey," there was a note of urgency in his voice, "what would you think about my taking a job away from Edgewood this summer and not coming home till a couple of weeks before college starts next September?"

"Oh, Brose!" My heart seemed to fall deep into my tummy and lie there, heavy and cold. "What—sort of a job?"

"A darned good one," Brose told me. "Good pay, interesting work, quite an unusual sort of experience. It's on a ranch in Texas. Jan Shelby—you remember I told you about Jan?—she's got it all lined up for me."

I just stood there, pressing the phone so hard against

"So was I," I admitted. But I went on then, trying hard to be sensible and not make things any harder for him, "Of course, you'll get back for a couple of weeks before school starts."

"Oh, sure," Brose said positively. "Maybe even three."

It would be too late then, though, a small voice deep inside of me warned. By that time a clever girl like Jan would have managed to crowd me out of his life completely. She hadn't got her father to offer Brose a job for no reason. There couldn't be that much of a manpower shortage in a big state like Texas. No, Jan didn't want Brose to get away from her, she planned to keep him right under her thumb, where she could work on him.

In a flash I could see the whole summer, like a Technicolor panorama. The long horseback rides, the camp-fire picnics under a desert moon, with Jan and Brose getting more attracted to each other with every passing hour. It was sickening, but what could I do about it?

"Tobey," Brose's voice sounded worried, "you're sure it's okay with you if I take it?"

"Yes, of course," I lied. I had too much pride to come right out and beg him to come back to Edge-wood, to me, where he belonged. I wouldn't stand in the way of his doing something I could tell he wanted so much to do. If only he'd never met Jan!

"And—you understand, don't you?"

"Sure, I understand." That, at least, was the truth. I understood too well.

The operator's crisp voice intruded to say, "Three minutes."

"G-good-bye, Brose." I gulped.

my ear that it hurt, while Brose went on to expl
He talked fast, so as not to run over his three minu
I suppose, and I didn't interrupt him. It seemed t
the Shelbys owned one of those fabulous Texas ranc
you read about, thousands of acres, thousands of cat
and so on. Jan's father always had to hire a lot of ex
summer help, so she'd offered Brose a job and I cou
tell by the way he talked how eager he was to take
Thinking of the selection of summer jobs available i
Edgewood, I could even understand his eagerness, a
though I didn't want to.

"But—you've hardly even ridden a horse." Was tha
plaintive little voice mine?

"That doesn't matter," Brose assured me. "Jan says
they do most of the work in jeeps anyway and, of course,
there's fence mending and all that. I wrote my folks
and they hate to have me away so long, but they think
it'll be good experience for me, so they said okay. About
all I could get to do back home would be tree trim-
ming or wrestling groceries at the supermarket. And
the pay would be peanuts compared to what Mr. Shelby
offers. But I want to know what you think about it.
Tobey? . . . Tobey, are you still there?"

"Yes," I forced the word past the aching lump in my
throat. "I'm here." I drew a deep breath. "It—sounds
like an awfully interesting job, Brose—but—I'll miss you
a lot."

"Gee, I'll miss you, too." I could hear the huskiness
in his voice across all those miles of wire. "But college
is so darned expensive, I feel I've got to help out." He
added unhappily, "Before this, I was figuring on all the
fun we'd have this summer."

"Good-bye." He sounded as if he might be going to say something more, but I didn't wait. I hung up.

In a sense, luck was with me. I made it all the way up to my own room before the tears pressing so unbearably against my lids spilled over. And Marilyn had gone out, so I even had privacy.

twenty-one

Home Again

ONE THING I WAS GRATEFUL FOR DURING THOSE FINAL weeks of school was that I was so busy I scarcely had time to think about Brose. I tried to lock and bar the doors against him and most of the time I succeeded fairly well. I laughed and joked and dated and didn't let my sister Thetas know that all my dreams and plans for Brose and me had gone down the drain. I knew, even after only one term of psychology, that this wasn't the wisest course. All the textbooks said it was better to talk things out with some trusted confidant than to keep them bottled up inside of you. But I had a sneaking hunch that if I tried to talk about Brose I'd burst out crying the same way I had the night he called me. And what good would it do, anyway? None of my friends could do more than try to console me, to tell me that Brose wouldn't get vitally interested in Jan, just because they were going to be thrown together all summer in that terrifically romantic atmosphere. And I wouldn't believe a word of it, so I might just as well keep my troubles to myself.

Suz was so happy because Dennis Bishop had taken her to an art exhibit and asked her to go with him to a lecture on Science and the Future that she didn't even notice I wasn't quite my usual gay self. I was just as glad. I took a secret pride in Suz's quiet happiness and hoped things would work out well for her. Better, I thought wryly, than they were working out for me.

Once when Dave and I were having Cokes at the Barn, he asked, frowning, "You feeling okay? You seem kind of subdued."

"It's finals," I fibbed. You can blame almost anything on finals and get away with it.

Close on the heels of our exams came all the pomp and excitement of graduation. My parents and Midge and Adam's father came to Central for the ceremonies. Adam looked very serious and quite handsome in his cap and gown. And Alicia glowed with pride. Of course, he still had medical school ahead and a period of hospital interneship before he'd be a full-fledged doctor. But college graduation was a milestone nonetheless.

There was still another week of classes for us undergraduates. Adam and Alicia went home right after graduation, of course, so I couldn't ride with them.

I moved through those last days of school almost numbly, so unhappy inside that it was amazing no one noticed. Even at the Thetas' big farewell party, I did such a good impersonation of a Girl Having a Fine Time that I fooled everyone. When I got home, I promised myself, I could let down a little. My own family would understand how I felt about Brose being gone all summer without my telling them. They'd try to help me have as much fun as possible and maybe, in time, I'd get over this sick stunned misery that made me feel only half alive.

The train trip from Central to Edgewood only takes

a few hours. The last time I had made it was when I had gone up to college for last year's Inter-Fraternity dance. Then I had been filled with expectation at the thought of being Dick Allen's guest. Now I speculated idly as to whether Dick might be getting home on leave during the summer. It didn't seem too likely, when he'd had time off at Christmas. And even the thought of Dick failed to cheer me up much. He was a good friend, just as Dave was. Neither of them could ever be more than that. Neither of them was capable of making me feel the way Brose could and had.

Maybe, I tried to tell myself, Jan wouldn't be able to win him away from me.

But I didn't believe it for a minute. All the cards were stacked in her favor. She had seen to that, or fate had seen to it for her. Not every girl had a father with jobs to hand out to any young men in whom she might be interested. Not every family had an enormous ranch to serve as a glamorous background for their daughter's romance. All the things I'd read about Texas floated around in my mind. The way the stars looked so big and bright it seemed as though you could just reach up and pick them. The way the moon hung low and campfires glowed like jewels in the darkness. The incredible loveliness of the desert flowers. I could just see them, stretching away in a colorful carpet all around the horses ridden by Jan and Brose. She would look absolutely beautiful in close-fitting riding pants and a wide brimmed hat, a bright scarf blowing at her throat. And Brose would be dressed just like the hero of a Western movie. Their horses would move along very close together, I thought, so that Brose could hold Jan's hand the way he used to hold mine when we walked home from high school. And then they'd come to a little lazy brook and dismount to let their horses drink the clear cool water. And Brose would kiss Jan. I could see him doing it quite clearly against the uninteresting, flat farm landscape sweeping past the train windows. I shut my eyes, trying in vain to escape the hateful sight.

The conductor called, "Bridgeville," and I opened my eyes with a start. Edgewood was the stop after this one. The scenery outside the window looked vaguely familiar. Brose and I had driven along that road when we'd been going to high school football games in neighboring towns. Brose and I—there was pain in the very memory. Would it be like this all summer, I asked myself, with everything I saw or did reminding me of him? I wasn't sure I was going to be able to stand it.

It scarcely seemed worth while to powder the shine off my nose and put on some fresh lipstick. But I did it out of habit. I straightened my stocking seams and slung my short yellow coat across my shoulders. Then I got my bags down from the rack. By that time the train was slowing for Edgewood.

As I stepped down onto the familiar graveled platform, the sun broke from behind a cloud bank almost blindingly. I squinted a little against the sudden stab of brightness and peered around for my mother.

"Tobey—" incredibly it was Brose's voice just behind me.

I swung around unbelievingly, staring, my mouth dropping open in astonishment. It was Brose. He had on a wild plaid sport shirt and tan slacks and he was grinning down at me, holding both my hands so hard it hurt. But I wouldn't have had him stop for anything. He could squeeze them till they dropped off for all I cared.

Now he seemed to have an even better idea, though. He pulled me close into his arms and our lips met. The station platform and the din of the departing train and any other people who happened to be around all faded away as if by magic. Only Brose and I were left. But we were enough, we were all that mattered.

Any lingering doubt I might have harbored about Brose being real and not just a figment of my imagination, was banished by that kiss.

Curiosity boiled up in me, so that I couldn't seem to get my questions straight. "But how—but why—"

"Come on out to the car," Brose said, picking up my bags and heading toward the street. "We can talk better there."

When we were sitting side by side in the Gilmans' old car, Brose's arm along the back of the seat behind me, I demanded, "Now tell me how you got here instead of being a million miles away somewhere on a ranch in Texas."

"I got in last night," Brose explained. "As to why I'm here—well, I'll tell you, Tobey. I had Jan Shelby all wrong. I thought we were just friends, nothing serious. I thought she knew that, I'd told her about you often enough, but—I'll never understand women, I guess." He shook his sweet, confused head and I sat there, hanging on his words, feeling myself come to life richly and warmly after all my weeks of numbness and misery. "When she offered me that job," Brose went on, "or had her father offer it to me, it sounded too good to turn down. So I decided to take it, even if I did feel awful about having to spend the summer away from you. I figured it would be an interesting experience and the pay was so good—and when I called you—well, you sounded as if it didn't matter to you if I took it."

"What an actress I must be!" I smiled rather unsteadily at him. "I cried my eyes out as soon as we hung up."

"You did?" Brose sounded flattered and sorry all at once and his arm tightened around my shoulders. "Anyway," he continued, "it was the darndest thing. As soon as Jan thought I'd be working there on the ranch all summer, her whole attitude changed. The way she started acting," Brose's voice grew resentful at the mere memory, "you'd have thought she owned me. If we'd been engaged, she couldn't have been more possessive. Telling me what a good idea it'd be for me to learn ranching from the ground up, getting sore if I even kidded a little with another girl, taking it for granted we'd be getting married later on—boy, did I tell her off! So then we had a big fight—"

"And she fired you?" Laughter bubbled up in my throat.

"I quit the fool job before she had the chance," Brose laughed, too. "There's just one girl I have any intention of marrying and Jan Shelby knows it now."

"I'm glad," I murmured.

"I may not earn enough this summer to take her places that cost much money," Brose told me, his eyes very direct and meaningful on my face, "but at least we'll be together."

I sighed. I couldn't remember ever having felt so

happy in my whole life. So happy and so sure and without the slightest doubt about my feelings and the future. It was wonderful.

I leaned close against Brose's shoulder as I told him, "That's the important thing—being together."

THE END